Indecent Dreams

Indecent Dreams

Arnošt Lustig

Northwestern University Press
Evanston, IL

Northwestern University Press
Evanston, Illinois 60201

"Blue Day" translated by Iris Urwin-Levit. First published in slightly different form in *TriQuarterly* 45 (Spring 1979). "The Girl with the Scar" translated by Vera Borkovec. First published in slightly different form in *TriQuarterly* 50 (Winter 1981). "Indecent Dreams" translated by Paul Wilson. First published in slightly different form in *Formations* 1:1 (Spring 1984). Afterword © 1988 by Josef Škvorecký. *Indecent Dreams* © 1988 by Arnošt Lustig. Published 1988 by Northwestern University Press. First paperback edition published 1990 by Northwestern University Press. All rights reserved.

Printed in the United States of America

The paper used in this publication meets the minimum requirements of American National Standard for Information Sciences—Permanence of Paper for Printed Library Materials, ANSI Z39.48-1984

Library of Congress Cataloging-in-Publication Data

Lustig, Arnošt.
  Indecent Dreams.

  Translated from Czech.

  Contents: Blue day—The girl with the scar—.
Indecent dreams.
  I. Title
PG5038.L85A2   1988   891.8′635   88-3202
ISBN 0-8101-0773-2.—ISBN 0-8101-0909-3 (pbk.)

Blue Day

1

INGE Linge was on the small side, but if you'd seen her early last spring, training on the sports fields reserved for the *Wehrmacht* and officers' wives, you'd have said she was muscular. Her calves were rather short, her thighs firm and round, as if made of white india rubber. She was a woman whom life had not yet overwhelmed, and her arms were plump and strong. There was no fire in her round face; its freckled pallor, low brow, and hair brushed carelessly across her temples all combined to rob it of expression. A soldier once scrawled on her door: "When a woman is pale, look out for wormy," followed by a nasty word. That was why she bothered with physical training.

There were times when she dreamed she was the owner of a thriving house, with young ladies wearing cornflower blue cotton dresses with white collars; she reigned over them all and occasionally took one of the customers for herself, for her own amusement or just to chat. At other times, she dreamed of a house in Prague where she entertained her former German friends, just to show them how well a woman could get on in life. And there were times when she dreamed she was tall and well built, with the long legs of a film star. Her eyes were snake-green with dark lashes, playful and demanding.

Originally, Inge Linge had come from Magdeburg to work in the Prague Labor Office as a secretary to one of the Reich's administrative officers. She turned out to be ill-suited for the role of office mouse because of her temperament and faulty spelling. Nor did she show any enthusiasm for the job. She was not very popular with the wives of her superiors, either, and so it had been fairly easy for her to strike out on her own at the beginning of February 1943. The German Reich was in trouble along the Don or the Volga just then, trying to cross the river and then proceed across the steppes to occupy Russia.

The four-story house, Number 14 Chestnut Street, where Inge Linge lived in her office days—she had refused to live in the Regulus Hotel with the other German girls—had two lower floors intended by the builder to be expensive bachelor apartments. With its front of Swedish marble, the building stood self-assured among decaying palaces which were collapsing one after the other. The apartments were taken over by post office workers, tailors and shop assistants with large families.

Inge Linge had been given an apartment here in May of 1942, and just as she did not have to stain her hands or her green overalls with black and red ink for long, she did not stay here long, either. This was the time of great military victories, except for brief delays here and there along one of the Russian rivers. All she had to do at the Housing Office was mention the name of her friend, Major Detleff von Fuchs. From the very beginning, the slim, dark-complexioned major with the pimply face and brow had been her mainstay; he always treated her like a lady. He liked her because she gave him what he wanted without beating around the bush, and as with his barber and his tailor, he set aside time for her.

She was given a larger apartment with a southern exposure. The sun filtered in almost all day, and she could watch the children playing in the street in front of the chemist's. They would lean over the gutter, which seemed to them to contain secrets waiting to be revealed. Children were her unfulfilled desire. Now, though, they were strangers and called each other Ivan and Jimmy and Friedrich and played and fought every day until the blood ran.

This apartment had belonged to a Jewess named Ida Geron, who suffered from tuberculosis and had been sent away in January of 1942. Inge Linge had watched her move slowly down the hallway, stooped with the weight of the two bags on her back. The old woman's greed had punished her, Inge Linge thought, for trying to take the entire allotted fifty kilograms with her to the east. Only ten kilograms were allowed for hand luggage, and the transport authorities issued a receipt for the rest. Everyone knew quite well what that meant.

Without a word of farewell, Ida Geron had gone, disgustingly thin, dragging her feet down the stairs, her shoulder blades sticking out, with her old-fashioned boots laced up over her ankles like a bareback rider in the circus.

Inge Linge told Major Detleff von Fuchs that Ida Geron's apartment was empty. Then she asked if she could trade her own small apartment for it, lowering her long chestnut lashes as she spoke. Even before he replied, she realized he wanted to take her to bed immediately. Then she enjoyed one of those lovely days that made up for having been born to a barber and a mother she never knew.

She was delighted whenever she thought of the girls in their cornflower blue dresses with white collars, and of herself standing at the entrance where the door set in motion tinkling xylophone keys playing Christmas carols. She could hear herself singing with the chimes: *"O Tannenbaum, wie schöne sind deine Blätter . . ."*

Her life had been pleasant enough, like that of a grubworm warmly wrapped inside a leaf. And now—out of nowhere, it seemed to her—it was as if a gale on a savage river had blown that life away.

At this moment—it was May 6, 1945, the third spring she had spent in this apartment and the beginning of the second night of the insurrection, although the German High Command had declared Prague an open city to spare it the sharp odor of gunpowder—Inge Linge wore widow's weeds and sat in an armchair covered with black crepe. She turned on the radio. Whenever the 415 meter band came on, the announcer said the Allies were bombing German airfields. He encouraged the rebels to hold on.

The various news items were often contradictory. Sometimes they were so brief and terse that she shivered; other times they were so vague that she could interpret them any way she pleased. But the truth was clear: the city had taken up arms to fight the Germans, and Inge Linge was being forced to recognize that something had ended and something new had begun. Everything she'd lived through in Prague, everything she'd enjoyed and dreamed of, was now gone forever.

She turned the radio off. The bells of St. James's Church were ringing and ringing. The policeman who had been on duty had disappeared. Inge Linge's snake-green eyes were desolate. The women in the house had settled their accounts with her early that morning, before she had even managed to ask whether they were bringing her milk. In a few short moments she realized that Germany was no longer what it had been the day before.

The chemist, who not long before had looked longingly and vainly up at her, pulled down his shutters, had put on a yellow tropical helmet—the sort once worn by the German Afrika Korps—and came to tell the concierge that he was off to join the fighting in the streets. The concierge was only half-listening.

She slapped Inge Linge's face and said to her, while the chemist stood by, "You want to know what you are? A whore, that's what you are, stuffing your belly when we didn't have enough to keep body and soul together. You were drinking milk when our children had to drink cloudy, gray water. Sucking our blood, that's what you've been doing!" She thought more was needed and went on: "You go back where you came from, you know very well what for, you viper, you. Get back to your whore's nest and stay there."

"Leave her alone," the chemist said. "She wasn't the worst of them."

Inge Linge was still rubbing her unhealthy pale cheek; it no longer smarted from the slap. She didn't feel at all grateful to the chemist for standing up for her. The wonderful feeling of those quiet evenings filled with the ringing of bells disappeared; no longer would she be certain that someone would come. No longer would she have to open the door.

What happened to her now would be decided by the Regional Command and detailed in the circulars issued by the office of the Reich's Military Transport Inspector, with its headquarters in the Prague Subcommand in the Bohemian-Moravian territory. The generals with diamond crosses and orders pinned onto their chests ruled the fate of the soldiers moving across the Czech lands and, indirectly, also the fate of Inge Linge.

Inge Linge was sitting in the armchair with her playing cards spread across the table in front of her. She wondered what she would say to Father Hesmussen in the church of St. James if she were to go to confession. He had blessed the soldiers' arms while she was dreaming of her house and her business, and he had sprinkled holy water on the artificial limbs of soldiers coming and going.

She was frightened by her thoughts. Yet this was only the beginning. She thought of what she would say to tubercular Ida Geron—whose furniture had been taken away by the Reich secret police to the warehouse in New Town—if she were to appear at the door. Inge Linge had been disappointed when she'd seen Ida Geron's furniture: a wardrobe with shelves built over it, a glass-fronted pendulum clock, a table and chair, and a broken electric heater.

She had never even been to confession. She only went to church to listen to the music and consider which of the devout flock would be worth sinning with. Once she had heard Father Hesmussen preach.

He had said of a couple, "The two went forth together." Now it seemed as though she and that Jewish woman might have set out on the same journey.

Why had the other woman always been so alone? Inge Linge wondered. She thought of her several times, whenever she found something in the apartment to remind her. That spring day in 1942, for instance, when she'd been washing the glass panels in the door and had scraped off a tin container stuck to the paint. Inside she had found a scrap of mica bearing the Ten Commandments. Why were all the Jews she had ever known, like Ida Geron, bent over as though they were looking for something in the dirt and dust beneath their own and other people's feet?

Inge Linge got up and went over to the wardrobe: a double wardrobe with shelves for her linens. She was still attractive, despite the veins standing out high on her calves. Usually she swung her hips like a sailor, holding her head high and her chin in the air, her full lips parted and the wrinkles of her neck smoothed out. At this moment, however, she did not bother to straighten up, and her walk lost its charm.

Her eyes passed over the green overalls with the white stockings she had worn in the Labor Office. She turned to the shelf of cut glass bottles containing a sickly scent of violets, roses, and orchids to tickle her nostrils. She had never cared for the smell of men's perspiration as some women did. Only a day or two before she had taken an oil treatment for her soft, flax-colored hair. Her creams were arranged beneath a lid of walnut. She felt like a pharaoh's wife whenever she looked at her jars of fine Meissen china and chose "Astrid" for nights and "Flora" for the day from among the gifts brought to her by German soldiers passing through Prague on their way from Paris to Moscow. She preferred Helena Rubenstein, or the Argentine Elizabeth Arden from Madrid, or the English Max Factor 3, an almost theatrical makeup.

The blue-marbled shadows with the words "The two went forth together" took on the shape of the old maid Ida Geron. It was likely that no man had ever touched that woman's body. Even in fantasy, the idea filled Inge Linge with scorn; it was something she found hard to forgive.

There had been a time when, partly out of pride and partly out of caution, she would not say good morning to her. It would have looked too strange when she was wearing her green overalls and white stockings. But she had never done anything to annoy her either, although at that time she might have hurt her as she pleased, even killed her, without any unpleasant consequences.

Ferdinand Linge, her father, used to say that everybody on earth had one nose and two eyes; he had shaved whole regiments of faces and he'd seen plenty. He would add that it didn't necessarily mean that a German woman had to go marry a Jew or a Chinese coolie, but he didn't go along with those sharp divisions that got even sharper as the territory of the Reich grew larger. Once, an officer her father was shaving—a tinker from their street who had taken over a Jewish workshop—said to him: "There are eighty or ninety million of us, Kamerad Linge, and every one of us might know a decent Jew. But if we hadn't kept our eyes open and given them what-for, everything in Germany would be topsy-turvy before long. A Chinese coolie? We're from the same street, Mr. Linge; take my advice and hold your tongue and be glad your blood's as German as Magdeburg itself. Luckily your daughter's got a head on her shoulders and she'll choose the right man for herself."

She, too—dressed in these widow's weeds—had caressed many a face and knew that, roughly speaking, they all had a nose and two eyes, and one desire that took on many forms. Pure blood had nothing at all to do with it. What else could happen that hadn't already happened to her? Suddenly Inge Linge put her hands to her throat. So many people have died, she thought.

Inge Linge had always wanted children and now, for the first time in her life, she was glad she didn't have any.

It had been a long time since she'd had any coffee—not even on the A-1 German ration ticket she'd kept since her office days. Who could guess that the smell of it had helped to drown out the smell of poverty that clung to the old days? She could say: "I've made something of my life, haven't I?" She'd never worried about things before. She had learned to live with herself. She never sought revenge for the wrongs she had suffered.

Maybe that was strange; foreign women had felt better in the wastelands of the east. A sudden change was not always a bad thing— she had heard them say so more than once in the office and on the radio. A German soldier from a Halle dyeworks lost his duodenal ulcers when put on military rations. She had heard this from another solider who had served with the dyer in Odessa on the Black Sea. He talked of nothing else, as if there were nothing of interest in his own life. Before that, he said, the dyer hadn't even been able to eat minced veal; it reminded him of boiled babies. His family was glad in the end that he had joined up! Meat was rationed in Germany, too, and she supposed they didn't like his saying that it made him feel like a cannibal. In Odessa, on Revolution Square, which they had renamed Adolf Hitler Square, the dyer pushed Russian partisans into double cages and left them there until the flesh froze off their bones. Nobody had to bother about his diet anymore. Then, too, there was a soldier with asthma who joined the Afrika Korps under Marshal Rommel and started breathing as though he'd been given a new pair of lungs.

She herself would like to get as far away from Prague as she could just now, except maybe not to the wild Polish plains on the Russian border where the bogs shone with a copper light. The young Germans from Magdeburg told her about the light when they came through Prague, after getting her address from Jenny Burckhart. Even Major Detleff von Fuchs said something about it, as did many others who wanted to talk, no matter about what, and were afraid to talk to anybody else.

Ida Geron? Who did that woman have? Was she really quite alone? And then Major Detleff von Fuchs—she knew perfectly well that he had bought his "von" for thirteen hundred marks. The "von" made his racial origin sound safer, and nobody bothered to look into it too closely.

What Daddy used to say flashed through her mind, that some people are too proud of their conscience not to drown in it. She longed for something she couldn't express.

Sometimes she would receive food tickets from the soldiers, coupons for fifteen hundred grams of meat and artificial fats, and coupons for two hundred and fifty grams of butter. Once she had three years' worth of coal allocations. She exchanged two of them for vegetable and fresh egg coupons, which only German hospitals received in Prague. She recalled the smell of the Egyptian cigarettes smoked by Major Detleff von Fuchs. He liked the Spanish proverb that said that a man without money is better than money without a man.

One of the sergeants she'd had here, Gerhard Muller, could not get promoted to lieutenant because they said he not only behaved, but also looked, like a Jew. They claimed he looked like a rabbi. That was enough for him to remain a sergeant eternally. He had mentioned this once, rather casually, and after that had never talked about anything but the weather—as if there were no war going on. It seemed unreal to her, like something that had existed briefly and was no more.

She recalled the song Major Detleff von Fuchs sang when he drank and when he got what he wanted:

Wir versaufen unser Oma ihr klein Hauschen,
ihr klein Hauschen
Wir versaufen unser Oma ihr klein Hauschen,
und die erste und die zweite Hypothek.

Inge Linge wanted to know whether his grandmother really was a Mexican princess. Who knows? Fuchs would say with a smile. What was her name? Delfa. She had a seafood restaurant on a famous lagoon. Strangely enough—in Fuchs's case—everything agreed, at least on the map. Inge Linge didn't care if the major was a gypsy or a part-gypsy.

Detleff Fuchs was married, though not happily. She could tell when his wife had refused him; it darkened his mood, even with her. He had his own ideas of order, of his personal things, which he wouldn't change. He knew how to make her laugh.

To cheer herself up she turned on all the lights: the big chandelier in the middle of the ceiling—like three enormous ornamental chrome candelabras, upside-down—the table lamp in the hall, and the white bulb behind the aquarium. She stayed awake, hour after hour, prey to the anxiety she was trying to keep at bay with memories of all that had been pleasant in her life and all that belonged only to her own experience, which nobody could take away from her.

She rummaged through her memories as though they were a bowl of dried peas, and then she suddenly realized that what had once made her happy was no longer enough.

She trembled as if in a fever. Did that soldier who was cured make good use of his lungs? The night dragged on and the harsh light glared down on Inge Linge crouched in her chair, throwing a series of shadows, first sharp, then softer and softer. She was wandering along the corridors of the hour-by-hour Regulus Hotel or in one of the wartime nightclubs of Prague, the Berlin Bear perhaps, where Czechs were not allowed. Or she was in some apartment where a German officer had lived before making his way to the front. Or she imagined herself standing at the door, or sitting in this chair, opening letters from the front and reading words of gratitude. They nearly always began with the same words: "First, my warm greetings and fond memories," as if they had all been written by the same man.

10

Or she was watching the tubercular little Jewish woman, Ida Geron, with her hooked nose, and trying to run away all the way back to the time when she was a green-eyed little girl in the parlor behind the barber's shop. The shop and parlor were separated by a curtain, and she could hear everything that went on. Ferdinand Linge came in wearing his patched white barber's coat. "You're a Prussian on your grandfather's side and a Saxon on your grandmother's side, you little imp. You got that black and gold flash of Bavaria from me, but God only knows what you got from your mother! Those snake-green eyes, I suppose!"

Inge Linge had never known her mother. All she could get out of her father—before he fell as regimental barber in the lightning French attack on Paris—was that he himself had only seen her mother on the day she conceived, and again just after she gave birth. Then her mother had run away with a hussar. Her father never liked shaving Hungarian cavalrymen after that.

And then she saw herself running over the dry Polish plains and coming up against silver barbed wire. A German soldier had told her about the wire. He was barely twenty-one and he wept on her bosom. He said that out there in the east, in the General Government, there were chambers with showers which they called "baths of eternal oblivion." The people were driven in and then, instead of water, they were showered with gas. Soldiers were specially detailed to collect the clothes and shoes and underwear from the changing rooms, where the people had stripped naked, and to send the items to the *Winterhilfe* to be distributed. At first they used to gas and burn the people as they were, fully dressed, but then one of the big shots—Heinrich Himmler himself—had given special orders to strip the people first.

Her hands went to her thighs; her fingertips felt the texture of her supple muscles. It was better to get up and cross the room to the aquarium. Inge Linge believed that the little goldfish would bring her good luck. Most of her fish were yellow, red, and gold. Detleff von Fuchs would tell her that a goldfish was only a little carp with transparent skin. He told her that the Chinese had cultivated it already thousands of years ago. Gold was the blood of the fish. And it didn't bring good luck, but bad. Once he had brought her a Chinese silverfish. It was still swimming here. The only good thing about a goldfish, Fuchs claimed, was that one could predict the weather by it. When the fish lay or swam near the bottom, it would rain.

She touched her neck with her palms and the pads of her fingers. The throat is the first to betray age, or fatigue, or a woman's worries. She noticed that her ankles were swollen like those of a pregnant woman. Perhaps I look swollen all over, she thought. Who knows why?

She turned all the lights off again, including the three big candelabras hanging down in the dark. She pulled up the blackout curtain, opened the window, and leaned out, breathing in the fresh night air. The bells were still ringing.

The sound of gunfire came from far away. She felt the pavement below draw her out and down. If she jumped now, perhaps she would suddenly solve the strange puzzle. At the same time, she was filled with the fear of what lay below. She closed the window and sat down to her cards again.

2

Later that night Inge Linge heard the doorbell ring, a single note. She was crouched in the chair. As the sound died away, the door opened softly. Only Major Detleff von Fuchs had a key. Once he had said there were snakes writhing in her eyes. Standing in the doorway now, under the blue gleam of the corridor nightlight, was an unknown German officer. His tired face bore long saber scars and his eyes were a steel blue. There was no sign of his rank on the epaulets of his tightly belted leather overcoat. It was the sort of coat the U-boat commanders wore in the newsreel she had seen only the Friday before. For a moment she was afraid he might be one of them. He had a large paper bag draped over his arm that made him look like a tailor's delivery boy.

Inge Linge felt as though her heart had begun to beat with a different rhythm, and her blood had begun to flow backwards through her veins, causing her pulse to flutter. Her fear quickly became expectation and she was prepared to accept the arrival of this unknown man as a sign of change for the better, although he had not yet said who he was, where he had come from, and why he had come to her, of all people. Maybe the rebels weren't doing as well as the concierge had pretended when she'd left her alone in the apartment, or as well as the 415 meter band announcer declared when he urged the rebels to fight on.

In the silence and darkness Inge Linge could hear the man's

breathing. Even if nothing happened, she thought to herself, the spell of her solitude had been broken. She smiled. The man carried, in addition to the paper bag, a small attaché case. He looked around the room nervously. Then he shrugged and sighed. She didn't understand. Before she could say anything, he spoke.

"You must excuse me if my visit is inconvenient," he said in a heavy voice. "Major Fuchs sent me here. My name is Paul Walter Manfred zu Loring-Stein. I was military observer at the People's Court in Prague. You seem to be alone here. I should like to stay with you for an hour or two."

Her mind was busy with his complicated name. Then she realized it wasn't wise for her to loiter, endangering them both if any of the tenants appeared.

"Please come in and close the door," she said quickly. And then, "I hope nobody saw you."

"I don't think anyone did."

When he spoke, the multicolored saber wound on his face moved as though it were following his words. There were three scars, side by side.

"You are courteous," he said in a low, serious voice. "Today a German woman is like an island in this city."

Her reply was a hesitant, forced laugh.

Then he said, "We sound as though we had met at a dance, but things are worse." He probed her uncertain smile carefully—thinking that the rebels had grown stronger in the past forty-eight hours, and the Germans weaker—and then went on. "I belonged to the Tribunal presided over by Counsellor Dr. Johannis Danziger. He was transferred to Wiedenbruck and took the last Mercedes. I myself was on my way to Germany and was taken by surprise when bandits captured the railway station. You can imagine the rest."

"I never thought judges looked like this."

"What do you mean, like this?"

"Like this. . . ." She wanted to say she had expected a monocle and a protruding stomach.

"Is there any danger that we'll be overheard?"

"I don't think so. On the left there's a separate building, and on the other side there's only an old woman who has lived alone for several years now. The rest of the family appeared before the People's Court in '42. I don't really know why."

"Are you a member of the National Socialist German Workers Party?"

The question didn't surprise her too much. She realized at once that the emotion she had felt in him that first moment in the dark, before he had begun to speak and the saber scars had begun to quiver up and down, had not been real. He was a German, filled with fears like her own, a soldier, an officer, and a man. Wasn't that the most important thing?

Although her memory was not well trained to deal with names—this had caused her some trouble at the Labor Office—his name stuck: Paul Walter Manfred zu Loring-Stein. With the same horror she had felt when she realized how alone she was, she remembered that she was wearing ordinary cotton underwear. She had possessed the foresight, however, to have sewn on the labels from more expensive underwear she had bought in Paris. She was pleased, too, that Detleff von Fuchs had sent her a judge. Recently her visitors had been soldiers from the Hradcany Hospital.

"I'm all alone here and I was beginning to feel that it was more than anyone could bear on his own." Now that this man had come, the meaning of Father Hesmussen's words—"The two went forth together"—had changed.

The officer who stood looking at Inge Linge did not understand the light in her green eyes. He had too many other things to worry about to wonder why her nostrils were quivering and her eyelids fluttering. She was thinking to herself that she would almost prefer his "zu Loring-Stein" to have been bought like Major Fuchs's "von." Perhaps the mere fact of his coming had saved her life, for she was no longer alone. If that other woman, Ida Geron, had died, Inge Linge thought suddenly, it would be better, if she were really and truly dead, with somebody who could officially confirm the fact. People from the law courts could do anything; they had laws and papers and rubber stamps for all purposes.

It was a silly idea. She realized at once how foolish it was, but she still felt the wave of relief that had come over her when she saw somebody else standing in the doorway. "The two went forth together." Perhaps if there really were someone who could confirm it, her fears might disappear, too. She looked at the military judge as he walked past her with his right hand in his pocket and marched slowly and deliberately around the entire apartment, examining the kitchen and bedroom. When he returned to the hall, he looked into the lavatory and out of the little window into the ventilating shaft, and into the bathroom as well.

"Which way do your windows face? Into the courtyard or out onto the street? Would you mind pulling the blackout curtains down?"

She responded to both his questions by pulling down the curtains; meanwhile, he put his things down. He waited until she had switched on the light.

He must have been surprised by something his words had not expressed, for he remained silent, first watching Inge Linge and then the fish in her aquarium. There were black fish, and tiny transparent fish swam gaily around them. The ripple of the water made the green plants sway. The military judge's lips were set. Now that she was no longer alone, Inge Linge was herself again.

"I'll put the kettle on for tea," she said comfortingly, and knew at once that she was going to behave differently. But her quiet, boyish alto voice sounded oddly hoarse. She asked herself why she still felt so frightened.

She said no more, and set out the teapot, cups and sugar bowl, gifts from a Russian town on the Don. Somewhere out there, on that day of national mourning, it had all begun. Or was it on the Volga? She had always confused the two.

"Thank you," Paul Walter Manfred zu Loring-Stein said, and then he thought for a moment. "If you would care for coffee, and would not feel hurt, I have some with me."

She was filled with joy and the hoarseness left her voice. "The two went forth together." Wasn't this a good sign? This high-ranking officer had what she had missed before. He was a German, a man, and not an emissary of the revolution.

She was looking at the door leading into the corridor. She had two kinds of doors. One was a heavy wooden door made from an ash tree, painted white, with two locks, top and bottom, and with a chain she'd bought in a hardware store with a German name at the Old Town square. And then the door into the bedroom: two white wings just a bit broader than a man's shoulders, the upper panels made of milk glass with a horn of plenty pattern. In the center, like a transparent moon, was a ball resembling the crystal balls old women stared into.

"What do things look like out there?" she asked.

"It's difficult to tell. What do they say on the radio?"

"I've only heard the rebel announcer. They seem to be holding out.

It sounded as if there was some shooting close to his microphone—a nasty crackly noise. Rifle fire, or a pistol. Quite close. The announcer said they were fighting the tyrants. He couldn't have meant us, could he? You . . . or even me?"

"Can't you get one of our stations?"

"They say they have surrounded the houses from the Czernin Palace down to Kepler Street where there was a German machine gun nest."

Her direct, rather frightened eyes were now focused on the officer. He was still in his early thirties, she guessed. His hair was soft and light, the kind that never turns gray, and his complexion was fair, too. He was tall and very slim. She watched him bend over his luggage, his back curving in a graceful arch, the gray leather of his overcoat stretched taut, smooth and gleaming like the sea. He took the tin of coffee out of his case and handed it to her with military certainty.

She couldn't tell what he was thinking. The judge dropped his eyes and thought to himself that she might have suggested he take off his coat and make himself at home. He would have welcomed a proper apology for what she could and could not offer him if he had to spend the dangerous time here with this little Inge Linge after a hard day's work examining informers. She was only a whore who tried to look like a Niebelungen beauty; he would have to be blind in both eyes and deaf to the hoarse note in her voice, and would have to forget what Major Fuchs had hinted at when he'd sent him here, not to see that. Even on a desert island he wouldn't want to exchange more than a few words with this woman. But he tried to keep the smile on his face. He wondered what he'd do if she became too insistent.

"Shouldn't you take your name off the front door?"

"The people here know me, and they've settled their accounts with me already."

"Who lives in the house?"

"There are only women at home now, and they won't bother me anymore. They slapped my face this morning when I went out to get the milk, and called me names. I don't think they really believe I was ever a tyrant. I've never done anyone any harm."

Then she added, "Why don't you take your things off? There's nothing to be afraid of. Major Fuchs never lets anyone down."

The military judge still didn't move to take off his coat. "Isn't there anybody in that chemist's shop?"

"No, the owner got himself a gun and went off with the other men this morning. He had one of our tropical helmets on his head.''

"Fuchs said this was a quiet spot, but he didn't say anything about that shop. Won't you take your name off your door?''

"I don't want to open the door unless I have to. If you think I should, though. . . . They told me what they thought of me this morning, and they slapped my face, and that settles things between us. I suppose they've won, now, and there'll be courts set up to judge . . . but not me . . . I really never have done anybody any harm. I haven't got the heart to hurt anyone.''

She saw his thoughtful metallic blue eyes in the network of saber scars, and she couldn't be sure whether or not he approved of what she had felt forced to say.

"I didn't look out of the window until now, in the dark,'' she went on. "There was shooting quite near. I expect it was near the Regulus Hotel, but that was this morning. They've got all the arms that were stored opposite the police headquarters in St. Bartholomew's Street. That's why I think the men who went away won't come anywhere near us.''

Because the officer maintained his skeptical silence, her thoughts returned to that woman's hooked nose. And once again she asked herself whether it was possible to grant or withhold the right to live. Here, with an expert on questions of law, she could ask and receive the comfort of reply. Why should she go on worrying about something she couldn't help anyway? Wasn't it a great Reich, and wasn't it clear that the Reich had the right to use cruelty in order to prevent others from destroying it?

If only this military judge would take his coat off—she imagined him in the judge's cap they wore at the Special Courts—and if only he would bother to respond when she was making such efforts at conversation! It was easier to talk to people who were not so educated.

Now Paul Walter Manfred zu Loring-Stein saw that Inge Linge was by no means as calm as she pretended to be. His steel-blue eyes took in the droop of her mouth, the embittered expression.

"This should never have happened to us,'' he said. He was taking off his leather coat with its satin lining stitched in a diamond pattern. "It should not have happened at all. Europe was ours, from the Atlantic to the Urals. This should not have happened to us. It appears we put our affairs in the wrong hands. We couldn't be everywhere.''

It seemed to Inge Linge that the tubercular Ida Geron had gotten into her head, behind the snake-green of her eyes, that she was peeling the tissue from them and saying something in a soft voice which no one else could hear. The judge, too, was thinking of one thing as he said another, in a low voice: "There's no need to lose hope. We still have an untouched army a million strong. We'll still show them what's what, German fashion."

"Let me hang up your coat by my uniform here." And when she had put the coat away she said, "I have some rolls here, but they're left over from Friday."

Perhaps it would disappear, after all: that ugly living ghost with its hooked nose. The courts would need some confirmation. Paul Walter Manfred zu Loring-Stein spoke to her as an equal even though his "Madam" and his smile lacked the intimacy she anticipated. She was an expert in different sorts of servicemen. She had given hospitality to sappers, foot soldiers, gunners, signal corpsmen, and airmen.

She knew that gunners were hard of hearing, and that when the signal corpsmen heard there was something in the air that might spoil their leave, they would search the middle waves of the radio, since the Reich secret police had all the short and long waves taken out of even German radios. She knew how generous and yet how niggardly officers could be, how impatient they could be, and how quickly their interest waned once they had taken the edge off their appetites. Short gasps of happiness were all that remained of her first boss at the Labor Office. Their first task was to fight: soldiers fought and generals won battles. But both lost something through this, and had less time for love. The generals never came to her apartment. The soldiers were different. They covered their feelings with rough talk and ridiculing themselves and her.

She had never had such an attractive and well-educated man with her before. Soon she would be able to ask him where he'd seen service, whether he'd been wounded, what battles he'd won. No man would refuse to speak with ostentatious modesty of the risks he had run; no man would refuse to reply to her questions. He would tell her all about the law and the courts, crime and punishment, criminals and cases.

Everyone had something to be proud of. She had never learned to be anything else. She had never been anything but a woman. She was flattered by a visit like this, as well as uneasy and uncomfortable.

Paul Walter Manfred zu Loring-Stein had taken off his fine officer's cap and put it on the crepe-covered armchair. His hair was as gold as the sun, brushed smoothly and neatly over his narrow head. He did not speak for a long time, and she imagined his scarred, gloomy brow full of deep thoughts; she took his mistrust for cleverness. He saw that after his few vague remarks the corners of her mouth were turning upwards again. She was smiling at the wardrobe, where his magnificent coat hung next to her green cotton overalls, and at his peaked military cap, lying on the crepe-covered chair.

"You must have suffered a great deal," she began.

"Lock the door and we'll block it so no one can get in. We can push this wardrobe against it." Paul Walter Manfred zu Loring-Stein took a broomstick and broke it awkwardly in half; he put the pieces down on the floor and managed to roll the wardrobe onto them towards the door. His fingers were strong and white, with ginger hairs at the first joint. He waited for Inge Linge to lock the door and slip past him—so close that he could smell the creams she used and then he pushed the wardrobe up against the door.

"Do you see what I mean?" he asked. "Law is strength. That is the whole secret. Now I can make up for what I've missed the last three nights. We were sitting until the very last minute; there were about two thousand of them to be sentenced during April and May, their people and ours."

When Paul Walter Manfred zu Loring-Stein spoke his words seemed real, made of lead. Now his silence had the same quality. She imagined him standing in his judge's robes, passing sentence. It was strange that for no reason she imagined it all happening in a dark rocky ravine, and, instead of a black gown, he had on a bearskin. His tired eyes watched her. He really hasn't slept for a long time, she thought, and she felt sorry for him, as though there were no cruelty in what he said, in life, or anywhere in the world. The mess they were in had brought them all down to the same level after all.

3

The night passed slowly.

"You've got everything you need," Inge Linge assured him for at least the third time. "The men are certainly out of the building." The officer-judge's look brightened and in his eyes she thought she saw the one response that could touch a chord deep within her.

"Are you of pure German blood?" he asked.

"What do you mean, exactly?"

"Are you from Germany, or from around here?"

"From Germany. From Magdeburg."

She remembered the soldier who had made fun of the Russian armies: A single soldier puts a horse to a two-wheeled cart, loads the cart with as much munition as the little horse can pull, and rides for over forty kilometers on a road muddier than German fantasy can imagine. If nothing befalls the horse or the soldier along the way, what happens next? The soldier had laughed in his bed: They'll use up the munition, kill the horse, roast it over the wood from the cart and then eat it. She wondered how different this military judge would be from that soldier; they both had two eyes and a nose.

The officer-judge looked doubtfully at her for a moment. She turned on the radio, tuning the receiver in search of the 415 meter band. When she found it, the announcer declared that Prague was fighting well and that the battle had moved from the suburbs to the center of the city. She turned the volume as low as possible. Sections of the enemy army had surrendered. Whenever tanks were sent against rebel units, they were either disabled by Molotov cocktails or else they surrendered. "Attention, attention! Prague is fighting . . ." Then he said it all over again. She turned it off.

"What did they say?"

She tried to tell him briefly.

"Were your parents German?"

"Of course," she replied. "Do you feel rested now?"

"I am a lawyer and I like to have certain fundamental things quite clear. I am sure you understand. Where could I change?"

Inge Linge smiled. It occurred to her that whenever two people came together, it was always possible for something to happen between them.

"You can change here or in the next room." And then, "My grandmothers on both sides were quite in order."

"Naturally," he answered. "That was not what I meant."

"I was almost afraid," she began, and waited for him to ask of what, so she could answer that she was afraid he had really come to her apartment only to change clothes.

Paul Walter Manfred zu Loring-Stein assumed that it was his question that had startled her, and asked no more. "So they closed the chemist's.

That's a good thing.'' He looked at her with his gunmetal-blue eyes. Not a muscle moved in his face.

"The kettle's boiling," she announced.

He raised his pale, sun-bleached eyebrows. He was thinking how strange it was that he—a judge, an officer, and a historian—should have come here to this little creature of the streets to find a refuge where he could pause to consider his next move. They had not counted on this uprising.

Was it only a matter of days now, or even hours? Was it a question of which Allied army got to Prague first? He gritted his teeth. And if worse came to worst and the fighting drew closer to this quiet street where the half-gypsy Detleff Fuchs had sent him to hide, he'd stand at the window and fire until his ammunition was gone, as the Germans had done at Annaberg.

He looked around the apartment. The wardrobe stood against the door and there was a big empty space where it had been, with old cobwebs on the wall. Inge Linge slowly swept away a cobweb and squashed the spider.

Meanwhile, Paul Walter Manfred zu Loring-Stein had discovered all there was to know about the place. If things turned out as he was hoping they would, he'd be leaving as quickly as he had come. He wouldn't let this little whore, who kept rolling her eyes and trying to act like a widow, get in his way.

He followed the silent movements of the black fish in the dark green water. The tips of their dorsal fins broke the surface. The bright little neon fish swayed rapidly from one glass wall to the other.

Even if she'd saved his life—and maybe she had, who could tell?— still, he wouldn't burden himself with her. Nor could he give her any reason to think he might bother with her. At the same time, he wondered whether he could leave as easily as he'd come, and he began to worry about ensuring that he could. For the first time, it occurred to him that she might betray him. Should he make certain of his safe departure by performing as expected? A swine like Detleff Fuchs might saddle himself with her. Someone in the German High Command must have a cruel sense of humor to have put a man like that in charge of the Protection of the Reich German Women in Prague.

In 1941 Adolf Hitler had thought of turning Paris into a vast amusement park for the whole of the Third Reich, but it hadn't worked out. Nor had the floods that were meant to hold up the invading Allies.

Around Dieppe almost everything had drowned; beyond that, it wasn't so simple. Those were the great days when Hitler, the parvenu, still found favor with the German nobility, the army, and the High Command. A lot of things had happened during 1943 that might have turned out either way. The law had decided to wait and see and to serve in the meantime. The fact that all was not revealed before the putsch, but only afterwards, had confused things for everyone.

It occurred to him that he might be able to buy his security in advance. He suddenly wanted to win Inge Linge's trust; her look was bold and skeptical. He was well aware that a mistrustful person is never easily or completely deceived. If it meant she would have to do unpleasant things to get there, would she even try to escape to Germany?

The furniture was not new. He was looking at it with an appreciation he hoped she would notice. Probably Major Fuchs had had a hand in that, too. He was responsible for the confiscated furniture stores of Bohemia and Moravia, as well as for the Protection of the Reich German Women in Prague. He was grateful to the major for giving him this hiding place. But what if the fighting did spread to this part of the city? Had the swine sent him here deliberately to get rid of him? It might have been treachery, or it might have been the only way out.

He could, even today, have Major Fuchs shot without the slightest regret. He told himself that he must get some sleep.

"Are you sure the light can't be seen from the passage? Through a crack in the door, or the spyhole?"

"Yes, I'm sure."

"I have brought you a little present; I don't want something for nothing." He probably wasn't as sensual as she would have liked, and he wanted to make his intention quite clear while gaining her confidence in some other way.

"Oh, no, I wouldn't like you to think that of me." Inge Linge's reply was unexpected.

Paul Walter Manfred zu Loring-Stein took out a small jewel. She didn't see that his interest was elsewhere, and not on her soft white hands and this house with the black marble front. For a moment she forgot black-haired Ida Geron, but it was strange for how short a time. It occurred to her that that woman, too, had been young once. She, too, might have received a gift from a man. But the gifts given to people like her had always passed into the wrong hands.

"Does Detleff Fuchs come here often?"

"Thank you," Inge Linge managed to say at last. "No . . . I don't expect him . . . I haven't seen him in a long time."

"There would be no danger for him in this street," Paul Walter Manfred zu Loring-Stein said in a voice too detached for her not to hear another undertone as well. "This isn't quite the center of the city. Still, I don't think any insurance company worth its salt would cover us now. I doubt if we'd even find a judge to set us free. And if we get hurt, there's not even a bandage left in the chemist's across the way."

Inge Linge suddenly stopped wanting to calm his fears. "You said you wanted to get some sleep. You can go to bed."

For the second time he thought she might betray him. Were she and von Fuchs plotting against him? He didn't like her green eyes, reflecting, perhaps, her weakness. Every woman who was attracted to him wanted something. He had to resist her influence with every fiber of his will.

Inge Linge was silent. Had the jewel belonged to his family? Had he taken it from someone? He was a judge, after all. He dealt with the law and the courts.

In her mind, she saw again the inflamed eyes of the tearful soldier, and he was telling her how they sent everything home to Germany, even umbrellas, spectacles, artificial limbs, and gold teeth. He told her how they used coal shovels to pile up the heaps of children's shoes, and how glad he was that his little niece had been killed by a bomb. It must have been a mountain of children's shoes: white and blue and pink ones, with straggly laces.

But Paul Walter Manfred zu Loring-Stein was looking into the wardrobe again. It seemed rather too luxurious. He thought about how they had all been ready when the trough was filled to the brim with the loot of the special commandos.

The dresses were heavy with perfume. It made him feel a hundred times sleepier. Why should he restrain himself in front of this little whore? Why shouldn't he do what he wanted to?

He looked at Inge Linge. He took in her firm little figure, the knotted muscles of her legs, one crossed over the other. He looked at her calmly through his network of saber scars. She was a woman for hire, a saloon artist on whom all he said was wasted. Just as Detleff Fuchs would never stop stealing and whoring with anyone who came his way, so this creature would go on spreading her legs in the name of the Third

23

Reich—in the name of anything—for herself. His eyes had begun to smart. He was more tired than he had thought. He was thinking about the men he'd seen during the last several hours—the unstable characters, disintegrating people.

Did she have siblings? Was there illness in her family? He was thinking about hereditary diseases. He remembered the sleek, well-cared-for riding horses, and leaning on the fence to watch the slow, rhythmic movements of the grazing horses. Huge in the dense gray mist, they reminded him of the local farm wives, with broad buttocks and breasts and modest pride.

The military judge was reading her every motion, even though she hadn't batted an eyelash. He detested fat women and knew in the depths of his soul that if she were to appear before the court, she wouldn't have a chance. The way she was trying to seduce him, as if she were snaring him in a trap, insulted him. It reminded him of the scent of perfume that attaches itself to a man. He gave her a wry smile which Inge Linge immediately returned with one of her own.

She didn't know what the military judge wanted from her and turned it upside down: What would he not want? The judge's look slid down her neck.

He was feeling the tired energy of the woman before him. He didn't like people who had neither the ability to speak nor the strength to keep silent. Disgust and disdain were rising up inside him, forcing him to control himself.

"Do you think I could lie down without fear of perfidy, then?" he asked dryly.

"Of course." Inge Linge went to turn the bed covers down. She did not know what he meant by "perfidy."

"I want to be alone." It sounded like an order.

The corners of her mouth drooped. He was harsh. Why did he behave as though she were going to bite him, or as though he found her disgusting? Once more she felt guilty because of Ida Geron with her TB, and goodness only knew what had become of her. Now she doubted that sharp line of division which had once separated her from people like Ida Geron or Jenny Burckhart, who used to live in their street, or her father, Ferdinand Linge, as long as he had been alive and lathering the chins of all ranks and services except the Hungarian cavalry. She knew the woman had died long before; indeed, there was no need for anyone to give her confirmation of that fact. She still saw her as she had looked

24

that day—with the two bags no one helped her to carry.

"Naturally," she said aloud. "Here's your bed. Sleep well. I'll be in the kitchen."

She walked out slowly, as though she'd given up the battle, hurt and surprised by herself. He did not create the diversion she'd hoped he would. She thought about the officer-judge, and Paul Walter Manfred zu Loring-Stein let his eyes rest on the wall where the picture was hanging.

"Is that a Prussian general?"

Inge Linge looked around and nodded. The figure was wearing a blue general's uniform with broad red cuffs and a high stiff yellow collar that made him hold his nose in the air.

She went out and shut the door behind her. Perhaps it was all due to his fatigue. She should have realized it sooner and saved herself the trouble. He wasn't a pear hanging on a tree waiting to be plucked. If only Paul Walter Manfred zu Loring-Stein had tried to overcome his anxiety, had tried to forget it all, things wouldn't have been too bad. Now she realized that the officer-judge who was so coldly dispassionate would stay or not stay according to his own judgment. The bells had finally stopped pealing. Neither Father Hesmussen nor Herr Haske was likely to be asleep, though. Germans in Prague would not be sleeping. She felt like someone who wonders what parts of herself had been lost along the way, someone who stops wanting to go on.

She tried to sleep on the sofa in the kitchen. She feared rejection. Was it rejection? But instead she lay on her back and gazed with open eyes at the dark ceiling. Where did it come from, this longing to be with someone, even though the other didn't feel it in the least? She listened to what was on the other side of the wall. Paul Walter Manfred zu Loring-Stein was lying in bed but he wasn't resting. She could hear him tossing and turning. The house was silent. Number 14 Chestnut Street was not part of the Prague uprising, and suddenly Inge Linge was not sure that she was really glad of that.

4

Later, the judge saw how depressed she was and knew he ought to cheer her up. His head ached as he watched her cross the room toward the radio.

"I thought I heard someone tapping," Inge Linge said to explain her entrance. It was clear that she was lying.

Paul Walter Manfred zu Loring-Stein crouched a little. "When? Now?" The saber scars seemed to be moving across his face.

"It's been quite a while now."

"Did you hear it a second time?"

"No."

"Are you sure?"

"No."

"Couldn't you have dreamed it?" He was listening carefully now.

"Yes," she answered, suddenly weary. "I think I must have dreamed it. I can't bear to be alone now."

"Pull yourself together."

"What's going to happen?"

"We have to wait. And anyone who doesn't know how will just have to learn, that's all."

"Are we going to lose?"

"Certainly not, not in the long run."

"I'm only afraid I may not live to see the day. That's why I'm so uneasy."

She twisted the radio dial and wondered whether she would be able to hold out until the very end.

Then the 415 meter band came on the air. The announcer quoted the Flensburg German transmitter, saying clearly: "Germany has surrendered. After five years and eight months of fighting, Germany has given up the struggle. This announcement was made by the German Minister of Foreign Affairs himself, in a speech broadcast from Flensburg, Germany, at 1430 hours. These were his words: 'Men and women of Germany! The German Supreme Command, on the orders of Admiral Doenitz, announced today that all German forces are to surrender unconditionally.' Reuters adds that it is not yet known whether these orders will be obeyed by all the German forces still actively fighting. In Norway the Germans have surrendered . . ."

She turned the radio down and half-closed her eyes.

"For God's sake . . . you heard it yourself . . ."

"Calm yourself. There must be something else on. It could be a trick."

She remained standing in the middle of the room. With her green eyes fixed on the scarred face of Paul Walter Manfred zu Loring-Stein, she remembered the very first time she had been with a man. She hadn't been very sure of what she was doing. She didn't even know as much as Jenny Burckhart, then. She had stroked his thighs and felt him tremble, waiting with bated breath for what would come next, for whatever she would do with her gentle, sensitive, caressing fingers. When she'd realized how happy she'd made him, she felt happy, too.

It was never the same after the first time. There were moments when it came back to her, like a distant reward for much hard work, but it was never more than a feeble reflection of what she remembered. When she woke up the next day she wanted to sing, she felt so happy.

She watched the steel-blue eyes of Paul Walter Manfred zu Loring-Stein. She felt sure she knew him. She might have forgiven him the insult of the night before. She really was what the concierge had called her.

The 415 meter band, which was now her weapon, spoke up again as her fingers turned the knob: "The Allies officially announced today that Germany has unconditionally surrendered. The act of surrender took place at 1441, French time, in the small school which houses Allied Headquarters. General Kurt Jodl signed for Germany. Although Admiral Doenitz has unconditionally surrendered, it is probable that at the last moment Field Marshal Schorner will order his forces in Bohemia—"

The broadcast was suddenly interrupted and Inge Linge turned away, as though even the radio had let her down.

"Can you get me a glass of water?"

She said nothing.

For a second his eyes—narrow, steel-blue, and cold—seemed almost dead.

Suddenly she had to leave the room before she did something inexplicable.

5

When she returned the officer-judge was not wearing pajamas or his uniform with its green and silver epaulets. He had changed into a dark gray civilian suit and was standing in front of her mirror. He looked like the representative of a German export firm. His blue eyes were nearly kind. Tall, neat, with a polite expression on his face, he was quite different. Only the saber scars did not fit his new image. The paper bag in which he'd carried his suit had been flung carelessly onto the bed. The sheet was turned back, and from the bed came the sickly fragrance of her own perfume mingled with his warmth.

As Inge Linge gazed with involuntary admiration at the man, the insult of the previous day dissolved and sank deep down to join the image of black-eyed Ida Geron. Paul Walter Manfred zu Loring-Stein was wearing a plain sea-blue tie. He looked serious but refreshed. The sight of him awoke in Inge Linge the same longing that had over-whelmed her the day before in the kitchen. The longing was memory, an echo of a feeling long past.

"I get silly ideas when I'm alone too long," she said. "It's no wonder. I'm ashamed of it, though. How did you sleep?"

Her last words were spoken in a low voice. Her hoarse alto rang with anxious appeal for the warmth of human companionship and a strange fear that sprang from the fate of that other woman who had walked about this same apartment. "And the two went forth together."

"Thank you, I really needed to sleep," replied Paul Walter Man-fred zu Loring-Stein. He looked around and said, "I like your flowers. I like flowers."

She looked with appreciation at his fine, tall figure. She knew only too well that there were not many men like him left now. She understood the situation in her own way. She felt grateful to him for being more accessible. What did she expect from a man at a time like this? Under-standing, coddling, the return of affection, or at least the sharing of it?

Inge Linge felt like going to him and stroking him. She trembled seeing the gleam in his blue eyes and the saber scars. She wanted to soften him for herself. She had misunderstood him.

Paul Walter Manfred zu Loring-Stein was thinking that nothing was sacred to a woman like Inge Linge. She did not share the concern that occupied the men and women of Germany at this dreadful moment—the loss of the rights and power of the great Reich. You whore, he thought to himself. He wanted to shout: Our great men are dying, and all you can think of is that?

"When the sun shines, as it does now, and the sky is so clear, there are wonderful blue days in Prague," she said. "I don't know why they seem so blue. Perhaps because of the bluish-colored roofs and the gardens."

BLUE DAY

"Blue days," Paul Walter Manfred zu Loring-Stein repeated thoughtfully. He wondered whether dark-skinned Detleff Fuchs made sure that women like Inge Linge were inspected thoroughly and often by an army doctor. Fuchs ought to hang, according to the canons of military law. The deep-set eyes darkened. The face with its mobile scars flushed. Maybe even her blood was bad for transfusions for wounded soldiers.

"Have you got someplace I can burn my things?"

"No," Inge Linge said. "Major Fuchs had everything wired for electricity. He was afraid of gas and open fires. I haven't got even a cellar here. I gave it up to the concierge. It's a big family, three men. They all work on the trolleys."

"Could you hide these for me then?"

"There's only the cupboard. I could put them way at the back."

He was reconciled to the fact that beneath that fair hair, carelessly loose about the temples, her head was empty and her snake-green eyes were without intelligence.

"Hide it somewhere," he said. "You know how important that is just now."

She felt the need to turn the light out. It was sudden and obvious. Everything was mixed up in her head—a head so round that German officers always said her mother must have come from Bohemia, or at any rate from Upper Silesia, where everything was so mixed. But certainly not from Germany. She turned the center light off and left on only the little white bulb behind the green aquarium. Flat-colored fish were swimming about, slowly and lazily. As long as she'd been able to buy fresh ants' eggs every day, they'd avoided the big black fish, but now they came out of hiding even during the daytime. They wanted to be as near the surface as possible when she sprinkled food for them. Now they were all starving and would be lucky to survive until dawn.

Once again Inge Linge saw the image of that woman floating there, the woman who once breathed the dry air of this apartment and then, as the young soldier had said, had been frightened by a final, bitter smell. Inge Linge reproached herself. She shouldn't think about it, if only because she was sitting here alive, with a well-built man, drinking tea. Because she existed at all, separate and apart, since there was no hope of union with anyone else.

She switched the radio on. It was her comfort, her weapon, and a challenge to him to stay with her.

"Who lives next door?"

29

"The men have all gone, and on that side there isn't a man, anyway. I told you so. They were arrested and never came back. I'll keep the sound low."

Sarah Leander was singing softly on one of the stations. Inge Linge knew the words to the song. She half-closed her eyes and watched Paul Walter Manfred zu Loring-Stein. How many men she had held in her arms, good God! Even if they hadn't all been his sort exactly, with his fancy name—as long as he hadn't stolen it, of course, or made it up. Would he really be as well-bred as he pretended to be if they ever got into a tight corner? She knew very well that his kind of breeding encouraged generosity when there was plenty, but meanness when bad times came. What sort of breeding was it, though, that required a man to withhold himself when there were thousands of reasons not to? It was a pity the major had not come. He wouldn't have left her comfortless at a moment like this. The singer finished her song and the dance music played on softly.

"Are the walls here so thick that you can be so lighthearted?"

"You can't hear through them. I've tried. You can believe me."

"Whether I believe you or not isn't the point."

Inge Linge was becoming more and more conscious of the silhouette of the man facing her, as though her breathing helped her feel him more clearly. She sat politely drinking her tea, watching his dark eyes with their metallic gleam. She felt a new wave of excitement pass over her. He really does have a fine figure, she told herself again, ready to devote complete attention to careful scrutiny of his person, even his saber scars. She wished simply to drown the fact that they were afraid of each other, the two of them, like dogs and cats, or cats and rats. Then a new fear swept over her, an anger, and a sense of expectation.

"It was a funny sort of day today. I couldn't sleep."

She couldn't help thinking again of the woman with the shriveled breasts. Where was the Jewish woman's grave, if she had one at all?

For women such as this one, Paul Walter Manfred zu Loring-Stein thought, for women who lived in hotels that had become dormitories in the hostile, conquered territories, German soldiers had stolen. They stole towels, silverware, lacy lingerie, napkins, pillows. Sometimes they used ships, which became transport vessels for the stolen goods. Others who had the opportunity and who couldn't withstand the temptation stole diamonds and rings for them in camps. He had only to look around the

30

apartment to get the full picture. He grinned to himself. There was no need to reach deep into his memory to recall other such cases he'd judged. The war had become an opportunity for many. His eyes were cold and held a sense of distance.

"It's night," she said to fill the silence. "The morning will come." Didn't Detleff von Fuchs sometimes say that you should protect yourself from those for whom you'd done a favor? Had it been perhaps something other than kindness that led him to send this man to her place?

She thought of the spring, which she'd always liked better than the fall; she thought of the way spring changes so much, everything changes from the ground up. Daddy shaved men in the street and told them: The worms in the cheese are made out of the cheese itself. She wished her father were closer. She thought of fish and swallows. Of the church and prayers. She was afraid of the night, of all that she would hear in the darkness.

She remembered what two Italian soldiers who had come here together had told her right away, in order to give themselves courage: The secret sin is a sin halfway forgiven in advance. The Italian soldiers were different from the German soldiers. They acted like people who had come by mistake to a different coffeehouse and, since they were already there, would order coffee or wine; but one could see that they'd be more comfortable someplace else. Those two Italians had laughed and said that to pray and to sleep are the same thing.

"I want to be practical."

"Of course. We both have to be practical."

"I don't want to be obnoxious."

The military judge didn't answer that. In her eyes he caught flashes of the instinct for self-preservation.

The military judge looked at her. What did she know of the People's Court passing death sentences for everything, including so-called nothings? He had learned a long time ago to read with a sixth sense the slightest gesture and facial movement of every person. He had inside him a map of his own world that also measured time; he wanted to spend it as he wished, not according to other people's demands. His mind selected, identified, accounted and classified. He would weigh and measure the wind and the stillness if he could. He had in him a compass he retained and which he would never give up. He felt

31

connected with something of a higher order than what was incarnated by this plump little whore, with whom he had to share his company. Innocence made his skin crawl.

"I'm glad you are here with me," she sighed. "I wanted to tell you last night that there was no need to give me anything. Maybe you have someone at home who could use the ring."

"It's out of the question. I know what I'm doing . . . assuming that I stay here, of course. It's dragging on and you didn't expect that it would."

"Thank you, thank you very much . . . that's not what I meant, though." Then she added resignedly, "That's not why I said it."

6

For supper Paul Walter Manfred zu Loring-Stein sacrificed two tins of Portuguese sardines. Inge Linge opened a jar of peaches and a jar of Italian apples. The officer-judge thought again that Detleff Fuchs, who had humbugged the Racial Office, had never had any use for military inspection. And undoubtedly he had sent doctors anywhere but here, where they were most needed.

"I've never been alone here for so long. I always try to be brave. In a little while they may start shooting again."

"What would you say if somebody did turn up?"

"I just wouldn't open the door. I couldn't, anyway, the wardrobe's in the way. But even if I could, I'd say you were a friend of mine, Colonel."

Then she watched him slip the safety catch on his pistol and put it back in his breast pocket.

"I like having visitors," she said. "Visitors from Italy were always the nicest." But that was not what she'd wanted to say. She thought of one flier who was killed in an aerial accident near Rome, where he was later buried. She recalled how the first time they had gone into her bedroom it had been dark except for light from the streetlamp that filtered in between the curtains. Though he had seemed passionate, he had taken the time to remove and fold his uniform carefully, draping his trousers on the chair. He had the legs of a girl. He began at her ankles and left a wet line along the length of her body. She had been told by a friend of his who'd later come to her about his remains, which were interred in the Christian cemetery. The other pilot had also been lost, in the Naples area; his body was never found. She looked at the military judge and wondered to herself: Are women more aggressive physically than men?

As she helped herself to more biscuits, her fingers brushed his. She felt him withdraw a little. She touched him again, and again she felt an almost imperceptible withdrawal. Where was it written that the man must be the aggressor? Women were better suited to that role. The old excitement rose inside her again.

Softly she began to sing in a hoarse voice that couldn't compare with the voice of Sarah Leander. What else was in the air? What did Sarah's song echo? Flensburg was silent now.

"Do you like sitting here like this?" she asked softly. Her lilac perfume was strong.

"Sometimes," he admitted. "Of course, I have a mission to fulfill, even if I am here with you. Yes, it really is nice here."

He spoke with cold brevity. And as his mouth opened to say something, anything at all, and the saber scars moved in their own way across his face, in his mind his voice was quite different. What an impudent little whore she was, indeed. Maybe she'd like it if he hit her. Adolf Hitler had been dead a week. And here he was, sitting somewhere in Prague, resisting this woman's solicitations. Maybe she would enjoy being beaten.

He would have to go on being careful. Inge Linge was persistent, and he could not push her away rudely, like a cow on a country lane. Nor could he sentence her for undermining military vigilance, particularly since he was wearing neither his judge's robes nor his officer's uniform. Perhaps she no longer felt herself tied to the German cause. After all, the concierge had considered the matter settled with a couple of slaps and a few curses. He needed this refuge for a while. If it had to be, he would just close his eyes.

"Shall I make the bed again?" Inge Linge asked. She knew for certain now that she would have her way, and she held her own with soft music and warm breezes.

"A little later," replied Paul Walter Manfred zu Loring-Stein, officer and judge. "I must finish my tea first."

33

7

Then Inge Linge was lying beside the officer-judge. She was still wearing a dressing gown, made of Japanese silk in a bright green floral design, the best her wardrobe had to offer.

"The bottles are all empty," she said apologetically. "I haven't got a single drop."

"It doesn't matter," he said.

He was looking at the empty bottle with complete indifference. They were strangers. She felt the urge to pick it up and fling it at his steel-blue eyes, which were full of disgust, and at his scars, to reduce the distance between them. She had before her the proud, tight-lipped mouth of an officer-judge, smelling faintly of aftershave lotion.

Yes, she thought, she was only a slut from whom anyone might turn in disgust.

Paul Walter Manfred zu Loring-Stein, although thinking more of himself than trying to fathom what was going on in Inge Linge's mind, nevertheless dimly realized what had happened. His scars were set in motion again. Her green eyes, full of distress at all the questions to which there were no answers, gazed at him, and her chestnut lashes were moist. Her complexion was pale, almost white, milky.

"I'll go and lie down in the other room."

"Why should you?" he asked. After a moment he said, "I would be better company, I suppose, if I had come to you under different circumstances."

As suddenly as she had decided to go into the next room, she now felt pity for him. Then that, too, passed away as he bit his lips, slashed and scarred in two places. Her old anxiety, driven by anger, threatened to return.

"Were you ever wounded?" she asked the military judge.

"No," he answered. "Why do you ask?" And then, "Do you think that's why . . .?" And he laughed deep and loud, as if he were laughing to himself about something else. It really meant nothing at all to this slut that the finest soldiers had been put to mending the streets. "No, I'm just preoccupied with other worries."

It was a lie. And yet what was worrying him most of all was how to get out of this lacuna of German law and order. It was taking longer than he had thought it would. For Paul Walter Manfred zu Loring-Stein would really not have enjoyed mending the streets of Prague, all dirty, his head shaved, dressed in rags.

Inge Linge felt somewhat relieved that her guess had been so near the mark. She felt a grain of superiority and the seed of a new cunning.

Paul Walter Manfred zu Loring-Stein, turning from his own thoughts, wanted to talk to her. Was he afraid even of this tramp? Was she capable of joining the bandits and betraying him? It was most unpleasant. His thoughts returned to mending streets.

"What are you thinking about?"

"Nothing in particular."

"What are we going to do?"

"We can only wait."

Could he take her with him if she asked him to? How would he get rid of her if he did? Inge Linge realized that the officer and judge Paul Walter Manfred zu Loring-Stein would never take her with him so that she could find Jenny Burckhart in Magdeburg, Number 29 Gotschal Street. He was afraid, just as fine ladies were afraid of everything that was rough, and as many of the men she knew were afraid. Again she was hurt. Under the metallic gaze of his eyes, she recoiled. Her warm breeze had chilled. She wondered whether it was really the way she thought, and she decided it was. Meanwhile, Paul Walter Manfred zu Loring-Stein lay at the very edge of the bed and felt that even that was enough to infect him.

"Would you like to go to the bathroom?" Inge Linge asked scornfully. She felt like a cat that had just spat. She realized she was being unkind but felt relieved that she had said something.

"Why? No, thank you."

Her first upsurge of anger receded, and with it the distant waves that had been rising and falling. Her green eyes, dulled and inflamed by lack of sleep, conjured up again the image of Ida Geron.

"Tell me something about yourself."

"That would be very boring," he said. "I was a soldier, a judge, I fought for Germany, and now I am a civilian."

"You will always be a soldier, even without a uniform, after the moths have eaten holes in it and it's become a dust rag."

"It will never become a dust rag!" he said sharply. He sat up on the bed. "Despondency does not become German women. Never, never dust rags."

"There was a soldier here once who did nothing but weep in my arms."

"What has that got to do with it?"

"He told me about a camp. I can't remember everything he said. I've got such a bad memory. He said there were showers, and men and women and children went in and nobody ever came out. All he had to do was open cans marked I. G. Farben. He checked every can off on a slip of paper and then he handed it in for them to send to Berlin. They were awfully strict about his checking every single can. Do you see? He had been a parachutist before, then he was demoted to the infantry. Perhaps his nerves weren't good enough for the parachutists. He didn't say exactly. Is it true what he said about those showers?"

He noticed her green buttons which looked like little rainbow flies in the faint light. The buckle on her bathrobe reminded him of a cobweb.

When she saw he would not answer, Inge Linge felt anxious. She wanted to relieve her feelings, to stop them from constantly whirling around in her mind. For the first time she thought that he might kill her. She no longer worried about what he might say next. He was still sitting up, leaning back on his elbows, the scars on his face twitching. Inge Linge lay quietly in the bright green Japanese kimono with her hands behind her head. The officer-judge watched her intently.

"A Jewess used to live in this apartment." Now it sounded terribly distant, the idea of the tubercular, dark-haired Ida Geron. "In 1942."

It must have been a long time ago, nineteen hundred and forty-two. Yes, she, Inge Linge, had the portrait of a Prussian general hanging here, nearly a hundred years old, and someone had given it to her, and his chin hadn't had been shot away. And the story ought to go on with more Czech heads, just as the judge had said so convincingly. Some shot-away chins her father had lathered with snow-white soap. Paul Walter Manfred zu Loring-Stein, Doctor of Law, was much more sure of his ground there than in bed; he must know what he was talking about. And somewhere, someone was smiling happily at it all. Inge Linge thought of the concierge's head, downstairs, and the heads of the three men of the family with the flat workmen's caps. And if that Jewess were ever to come back, her head, too.

Inge Linge looked at his gun.

"There's nothing to be frightened of. I will protect you."

"I told you I wasn't afraid anymore."

"We can only expect the worst from the people downstairs who tried to beat you up. Be glad you've got me here with you and that we aren't unarmed." Again he paused before saying, "Let me tell you something, my dear."

Inge Linge watched his lips and knew that Paul Walter Manfred zu Loring-Stein was talking to her only because he had no other audience.

"Now listen," he said. "The rebels aren't likely to send dead men where I want to go, so we must do all that we can to get out alive. First I, then you." He fell silent again, disappointed that Inge Linge had not cried out enthusiastically.

Then he said dryly, "How long have you been living here—five years? A plague on this filthy city. The courts couldn't send more than a hundred to the wall each day. Don't you know what these Czechs are like? Only the most aged collaborated with us. Even though I hate them, they're like young trees full of sap and the juice of life. They were bent to the ground but they didn't break. You can stamp on them, but they spring up again, unless you shoot them in the head to make sure they're finished. It's a good thing these bandits aren't Germans, as we originally planned for the better specimens. They would have made bad Germans. But the time will come when they'll all be dead, anyway. Do you know how to use a Steyer?"

"What is it?"

"A pistol. My reserve weapon."

"No, I don't." And then: "I never bothered about such things. That's why I'm where I am, I told you."

There was a desolation within her, a graveyard in her heart. She was no longer listening to Paul Walter Manfred zu Loring-Stein. In her mind she was putting flowers on a grave, and the words of Father Hesmussen took on a new meaning. White lilies and hyacinths and red roses—not only for herself. The thousand perfumes in her bottles in that cupboard, and her underwear, artificial silk and real muslin, her beautiful dresses, and Ida Geron who had lived here before her. Inside of her, there was no trace of anxiety, nor of hate.

"They say we have done terrible things," she said.

"We only did what others would have done in our place. That, of course, is the legal way to look at it. Now we are sent to mend the streets. It's a good thing we did what we did. Fear inspires respect. They had to be shown who they were dealing with—that for each one they killed, others would come, worse, more brutal, more ruthless. Don't try to look innocent! Every child knows about the liquidation squads. That was what your befuddled parachutist was talking about. I would say he didn't deserve to be demoted to the infantry; he should have been hanged outright. You can soothe your conscience, though. We were never as thorough as the world would like to think.''

"So it is the truth."

''What do you mean, 'the truth'? Czech truth? Or even Jewish truth?''

"I mean the baths and showers."

"Have you seen them with your own eyes? You haven't? Everyone should be asked that when he starts asking impertinent questions. What you haven't seen doesn't exist, do you understand?'' Then he laughed. ''My dear Inge Linge, perhaps this isn't the right moment for what I am going to say to you. When those who survived our baths and showers grow up, they will be astonished at how mild we were—as mild as lambs. Relax. Where there is no evidence, there is no crime. And in a few years . . .'' He paused. ''Our German lawyers will know what to do and when and how to do it. There's no need to think about it all now, if it makes you nervous. Things weren't as bad as people say. Our camps were places of opportunity, after all, for our soldiers and the undisciplined units. We gave the strong a chance and the weak a way out. Everyone had an opportunity to show what he could do. Don't listen to stories. There are far too many stories being told. The strong will be grateful to us one day. The weak would have died anyway, without our help. Life is like that. The criterion of selection.''

And he was thinking that no one would have any interest in glorifying those who had gone to the gas chambers without resisting. He still held his pistol in his hand. She noticed once more his strong white fingers with the ginger hair.

"Chin up, now! There's no need to be sad, Inge Linge."

"They're still shooting."

"Yes, I know."

"I heard it while you were talking, but I'm not afraid now." She was wondering if the rebels would do the same things that had been done to them.

"You were always kind to them. There's nothing for you to be afraid of."

His stern, metallic blue eyes searched her green eyes a third time for signs of treachery.

"I'm living in a Jewish apartment," she replied.

"There are no Jewish apartments anymore, Miss Linge. It's as if, in addition to everything else, you let these people tie an iron ball to your legs."

It flashed through his mind how many people at this moment were begging for proofs that they had given to this or that Jew, communist, or lunatic, a ticket for a hundred grams of beef, a coupon for soap, or a train ticket to the countryside. Or trying to prove that they had paid a good price for Jewish furniture, dishes, or fur coats. The world was topsy-turvy, he thought to himself. People were confusing Germany with a whorehouse. He looked at her but was thinking about the German submarines. What are they doing now? Are they sinking enemy ships or taking their leaders to safety? German submarines, he thought: the best, the fastest, the deepest diving. What are they going to do tomorrow, the day after tomorrow, when the war is over? Are they going to surface? Where? Brazil? Canada? America?

8

She went into the kitchen, still filled with a feeling of desolation. She opened the window so that she could hear the men if they came back, and the shooting if it came into Chestnut Street. Night air filled the room. With strange deliberation Inge Linge set about her task. From a wicker hamper she took a little flag, a swastika embroidered on silk. She had been given this flag in return for her services by a nasty tank officer of the *Grossdeutschland* division, who had never dared to come and see her again. Leaning well out of the window, she attached the flag to a nail driven into the sill, left there from the days when Ida Geron had grown flowers in a windowbox. It took her some time to fasten it securely.

When at last Inge Linge finished, she stretched one hand through the window and felt a gentle breeze. She could smell gunpowder and spring and a new unsullied life. Perhaps the breeze carried the ashes of the black-eyed, black-haired, tubercular Ida Geron, and deposited them on the peeling paint of the window sill, so that the flat-breasted woman found a resting place at last. Inge Linge could smell it still. She guessed at a thousand scents when she laid the pistol on the sill by the curtains. She lay down in her Japanese kimono without a blanket to wait for daylight. The shooting came nearer, through Tyn Courtyard, where the Regulus Hotel was, and around St. James's Church. But Inge Linge no longer recalled Father Hesmussen or the pealing tones of the organ. The pistols and the Steyers and the grenades sounded closer and closer.

An hour or so before daylight, Paul Walter Manfred zu Loring-Stein looked in. She told him not to switch the light on because the window was open so that she could hear better. He looked suspicious.

"The two went forth together." It sounded like a slogan.

"I'm glad to see you are being sensible," he said. "Keep the pistol with you." The scars on his face looked almost purple.

She trembled with fear that he might go to the window.

Instead Paul Walter Manfred zu Loring-Stein left the room with the uneasy feeling that although he had managed to calm Inge Linge, his method had not been best suited to this time of anarchy.

Outside the night mist still hung in the air. As dawn broke, it began to thin. Inge Linge waited.

She looked toward the window. She felt a strange, quiet anxiety that rose within her like a wave in the sea and then fell off and began to dissolve almost into infinity. Suddenly she couldn't recall the way she looked. It was as if she saw in herself someone she'd never seen before.

Paul Walter Manfred zu Loring-Stein was waiting in the next room. At the moment of daybreak, when the steel grenades came through the windows of the apartment where once a stooping Jewish woman had lived, Inge Linge thought that at last the night had gone and day had come. She knew the sun would be shining brightly, first red, then yellow, and finally white. The blue day was there in her eyes, but nothing else now: not light, not the breeze, not even the gulping of dying fish from the shattered aquarium.

The Girl with the Scar

1

WARM, muggy air poured into the classroom. The pale girl suddenly gave a loud sigh, clearly audible in the total silence of the room. She was sitting near the teacher's desk, in the front by the window, where she could see only the tips of the magnolias on the Superintendent's house across the street; she could just glimpse the soft blue of the sky. Her sigh had somehow slipped through the barrier of the heat. She had a little face, a long, thin neck, and a small body with small breasts. It seemed as if the silence had taken her by surprise. The heat seemed to spread under her feet like an abyss, as if the tremor of an earthquake had opened up the ground. All morning it had been building up inside her, like a pressure that might erupt without the slightest warning.

She was fumbling, somewhat listlessly and absentmindedly, with a narrow-hemmed scrap of beige handkerchief which she'd made out of an old curtain in sewing class. A long, narrow scar ran across her forehead.

"Jenny Thelen," the teacher reprimanded.

"Yes, ma'am," responded the girl with the scar.

"Is that any way to behave?"

The girl said nothing, though in the reprimand there was also the promise of pardon. She languidly closed her large, green eyes; they were like sharply outlined little boats lodged in the rift beneath her scarred brow, bordered at the temples by shocks of light brown hair. She tried not to hear the teacher's throaty voice, but it rasped against her like a wire brush.

She tried to return, at least in spirit, to where she'd been before the sound of hobnailed boots, husky voices, and shrill whistles had called her back.

She let the sun caress her, its rays gently touching her like fingertips. She could feel her chest being warmed by the sun. She thought suddenly of hellfire.

On the wall, next to a picture of a scene from German history—Frederick the Great and Freiherr von Stein—there was a quotation from Immanuel Kant, lit now by the streaming sun. She tried to return to the daydream she'd begun while Elzie Mayerfeld was explaining the difference between the borders of the German Reich and those of the Great Germanic Empire.

Sunlight was playing on the magnolias. Over the Superintendent's garden shed was a big circular sign that had been used during one of the spring gymnastics festivals:

WIR WOLLEN KEINE CHRISTEN SEIN,
DEN CHRIST WAR NUR EIN JUDENSCHWEIN

When she squinted into the sun, it looked like a great, golden recording of Johann Strauss's waltz *Tales from the Vienna Woods*. The disc seemed to turn silently around its blinding center, the molten center of the sun. Hell. She closed her eyes quickly, afraid she'd go blind otherwise. But even with her eyes closed, the light seemed stronger than when she'd focused on the sun's center.

She turned her attention to Elzie Mayerfeld's dress—tight, shiny silk with large red roses and green leaves. The teacher was swinging her hips and admiring the reflection of her tall, dark, supple body in the window.

"Let's go on, *lieblings*," said Elzie Mayerfeld. Elzie Mayerfeld—known as the Dog Lady—paused in her explanation of how the frontiers of the Reich would expand over the next thousand years.

"In the struggle between wealth and poverty, which will come in the next ten centuries, the conquered and impoverished nations will have themselves to blame and not the Germans," she said. "Think of yourselves. Think positively of your own personal contributions to the welfare of Germany, rather than about who's getting rich from the suffering of others."

Through the open windows came the clatter of hobnailed boots striking the pavement—countless feet stomping in unison, marching away into the distance until only the echo of shrill fifes lingered behind. They were singing about earth and blood and the distant Fatherland, about what it meant to be a soldier in time of great crisis. The hoarse voices from the uniformed throats merged with the strict beat of the marching boots: *Hei-di, hei-do, hei-da!*

Elzie Mayerfeld's nostrils quivered. Her blond hair was pulled back in a chignon, held in place with a big tortoiseshell comb. She had smooth, pale skin; with her hair up, her bare neck was long and white. From the distance, the fifers' whistles still pierced the air and drumbeats merged with the thud of boots. The sound softened, becoming a pleasant cadence. This was the fifth day of such relentless heat. The pavement radiated the sun's warmth in waves, making the city like a furnace. The facade on the Superintendent's house was peeling, and the sills looked raw, their eagles and angels naked. Elzie Mayerfeld thought of General Rommel and the German armies in Africa.

The hard thudding of the hobnailed boots, the scent of the magnolias, and the tender sea of heat on which sound and order floated all seemed filled with the meaning of the song. The fifes, the drums, and the words—as long as they could be understood—recalled the distant Fatherland.

As the soldiers moved away, the hot air of Prague's German Quarter flowed in. Only a rhythmic echo lingered in the boundless space over the roofs of Otto Bismarck Street. Looking at the slate roofs, Elzie Mayerfeld saw an image of blood and of strong male legs—of men who pushed onward and onward, night and day, through heat and wind, to all four corners of the earth. It was an image of weathered faces with eyes squinting into the sun, faces set against a background of demolished cities and burning villages.

The sun beat down on the windowpanes. Through the silk of Elzie Mayerfeld's dress one could see the outline of her underwear. She was tall, even without high heels, and taller still when she wore them. She smiled without being aware of it. Her eyes were shining.

"There will be nothing to stop our access to grain and oil in the future. Poland and Russia will no longer block us in the east as they have for the past thousand years." The Dog Lady smiled as if she were saying that all the wealth of the world—from east and west—would begin to flow through the Reich, just as rivers flowed in their beds.

She closed her eyes. She saw herself at the military parade, the music playing. She wished to breathe into the girls' souls pictures of the fighting soldiers, consecrated to death as nuns are consecrated to God.

45

She felt responsible for the girls, who evoked in her desires that were forbidden.

In Elzie Mayerfeld's smile was Germany itself: the Fatherland, surrounded by the islands and the rough rocks of a German sea. In the end it always came down to privilege, and the question of who had the strength and stamina to seize it, to take it roughly the way a man takes hold of a woman, even at the price of German blood. A German cannot live in the same way as a Jew, a Pole, or a Russian.

Finally, there lingered in the scorched air only the fading refrain of a song that Elzie Mayerfeld and the girls in her classroom remembered, about how, in the far-distant lands, a German soldier would know when his time had come.

Elzie Mayerfeld turned to face her students and said, "*Lieblings,* I have a surprise for you."

"She's going to give us a test," whispered a girl sitting next to the girl with the scar.

Jenny Thelen looked down at the floor. The wooden tiles were angled like swastikas. The Dog Lady had explained to them the very first day that the bent cross was not only the symbol of the great German Reich, but also of the sun. In the old Aryan nations it had also signified the union of man and woman.

Every time the Dog Lady called them *lieblings* it was like the sting of a wasp.

"I bet she wants to leave early," Jenny Thelen's neighbor whispered.

"Third row by the window!" The Dog Lady immediately noticed. "Don't disturb the class! Kindly take out your notebooks." She lowered her voice, getting down to the business at hand. "Write the answers to three questions." She thumbed through the morning edition of *Der Neue Tag* looking for the marked articles. "I'm going to leave you by yourselves for a while. I have to leave a little early."

"I told you so," said Julie.

"How did you know?" the girl with the scar asked in a very low voice.

"He's waiting for her downstairs."

The girl with the scar felt the blood rush to her cheeks. "Who?"

"You sound like you envy her."

"The third row's asking for punishment," said the teacher. "I'm not here to discipline you; my mission's more important. I'm telling you for the last time to keep quiet."

The same fragments of images floated in Jenny's mind, images that went back to Tuesday, to her thoughts before the teacher's lecture had been interrupted by the marching songs of the soldiers. So someone was waiting for the Dog Lady. It wasn't hard to guess who. Jenny had been thinking about the sun, about hell and the restful shade, but now she thought about victory. Defeat she pictured as a net made of fire. To her, there was no more difference between them than there was between a butterfly and a moth. She was no longer aware of the classroom, but her lips whispered automatically, "I beg your pardon, I forgot myself" — the apology that the tall teacher demanded.

Jenny Thelen was no longer aware of the battered desk or the big map of the Reich, nor of the silk dress or the magnolias on the house across the street. She shut her ears to the teacher's irritated voice. All that was left were the tiny motes of dust and the sun, the soft play of streaming rays of sunlight. The sunbeams were long, thin, golden shadows. She felt herself glide down them, her eyelids half-closed, as if she were drifting off to sleep. Everything surrounding her was real, and yet she was aware of none of it. Nothing remained but the light and the thing she was learning to forget here in the Prague Institute for Girls of Pure Race from Non-German Territories: that in the year 1942 she had had a father and a mother. But she had not yet learned to forget what it was they had been executed for.

Something was streaming through her subconscious, like mud drifting on the bottom of a river, something connected with the damp day of March 15, with its snow and the motorcycles ridden by foreign soldiers who wore green cloth tunics under their raincoats, reminding her of uniformed frogs.

Father was wearing the nickel-rimmed glasses he'd just brought home from the health insurance company (as an employee at the waterworks, he was entitled to a yearly eye checkup and new glasses). He didn't want to see what was going on outside the window, so he took the glasses off. He said it was a wonder that the occupation soldiers weren't singing. And at just that moment they'd started to sing— songs about distant German lands, about earth and blood, with fifes and drums: *Hei-di, hei-do, la la.* Tanks tore up the road. After that, Father had taken her on his knee more often and told her about the times when he'd fought on the River Piava in northern Italy, where he'd learned to play *O Maria* and other songs from Trieste on the mandolin.

Drops of perspiration appeared on Jenny's forehead and above her upper lip. She was hot and tired. She hadn't slept well the night before. She hadn't slept well since Tuesday. In the morning the Dog Lady had talked about what united children and parents and what divided them. The rays of sunlight bore down on her.

"I know who's waiting for her," whispered Julie. "It's him. I'll bet you anything. They made a date for Saturday."

"It's awfully hot," whispered the girl with the scar, as if admitting that it was a possibility. She no longer felt that she could see her mother and father in the rays of the sun.

She dropped her hands into her lap. The sun shone on the beads of sweat running down her forehead. Suddenly she had an urge to get up, without permission, and go to the window to see who was waiting for the teacher.

She felt a flush of shame and, at the same time, an insatiable thirst. For a moment her body felt like a big empty pitcher.

The open windows let in the smell of flowers. The fragrance aroused her and brought back all the excitement she'd felt last Tuesday. Again she remembered the Noncommissioned Officer's visit to Elzie Mayerfeld, and the touch, perhaps accidental, of his broad palm brushing over her small breasts. She must have blushed immediately, her cheeks turning fiery red. She'd felt the blood rushing to her head. Then she heard the NCO promising to wait for her after class on Saturday. He probably had no idea what punishment such a breach of the rules could bring. She'd smelled the slightly acrid yet sweetish aroma of tobacco on his breath.

"What do you say, lambkin?" he said.

She'd been glad when he'd left. Her heart had pounded as if she'd been running. But when he'd gone she wished for something else. The next day, Wednesday, the Dog Lady had made them line up in their gym suits. He'd been watching them from the Dog Lady's room.

"You two over there," said the teacher. She folded up *Der Neue Tag*. There was a long article in it about the Czechs that claimed they were more concerned with their standard of living than with their national goals. There was also a detailed article about dogs. Elzie Mayerfeld was well aware of what was going on in the classroom. She looked sharply toward the third row.

That was the moment their eyes met, those of the teacher and those of the girl with the scar. The girl's eyes held the teacher's gaze until they could no longer bear it, then moved to the windows and finally to the floor. The teacher again examined her face: the deep-set eyes, the narrow forehead with the long reddish scar that looked like a quickly sewn seam, her Slavic cheekbones, the pointed chin. An almost childish triangle of a face, it reminded her of a lamb's.

The scar turned pale for a moment. The teacher guessed that the tension inside this girl was not so innocent. The teacher's nostrils flared like those of a lioness. The girl knew that she could do nothing without permission, not even stand up and go to the window.

Everything came back to Jenny now—all Father had said and done when the Germans were occupying Prague. She felt numb, as if she were about to faint. Silently the words about the frontiers of the Reich echoed. *Alt Reich* and *Neues Reich*. In her fading smile, the girl felt the mature woman's disdain. She was avoiding Elzie Mayerfeld's gaze, but even so, she felt naked, as she did when they were measured and weighed, or when they were given blood tests.

"Keep your minds on your work," the tall woman admonished. "I demand silence, Jenny Thelen. It's not easy, but it's not so much to ask. Absolute silence. Voluntarily."

Finally she said, "Write as I dictate."

It took the girl with a scar a while to come back to reality. The sun was dazzling. A ray of light sparkled on the teacher's bracelet. She began to dictate.

"Question one: What's the *Curatorium* doing for us?

"Question two: Why must Germany—in the interest of Europe— defeat Bolshevik Russia, Jewish England, and plutocratic America?"

Elzie Mayerfeld folded *Der Neue Tag* on her desk. She smoothed her dress over her hips with soft, cushioned palms.

"Question three," she said. "Why is censorship progressive, when compared to the arbitrariness introduced in Europe like a Trojan horse by the Jews? What's the meaning of 'undesirable,' 'blasphemous,' and 'lewd'? How does the National Socialist German Workers' Party, the NSDAP, view the relationship between freedom and experience?"

The girls wrote the questions slowly, as she dictated them. Jenny saw the teacher's reflection now in the glass of the open windows. Everything about her looked full and dark; she seemed to exude an aura of animal magnetism.

"Now you may begin," said Elzie Mayerfeld.

Then she added that she expected silence and order in her absence. That's what obedience meant.

Elzie Mayerfeld's hips swayed. Her cushioned palms moved up and down the rustling silk, as if shaping her body into curves.

She said aloud, "I'll make it up to you. You won't miss anything. This evening I'll teach you how to waltz. Our soldiers are fond of waltzes."

She moved a few steps away from the desk. She wore another gold bracelet on her left ankle.

"There are three ways you can do the waltz," said Elzie Mayerfeld. "I have a new Lale Anderson record. She has such a wonderfully velvet voice. She's better than Marlene Dietrich used to be. Much better. She's also braver, of course. Lale Anderson's still our best frontline singer. I'll pick up your notebooks in the evening."

The girl with the scar found all this uninteresting and irrelevant. She was filled with a thirst that didn't burn, but that sapped the strength from her arms, legs, and brain.

Elzie Mayerfeld dilated the deeply sculpted nares of her long, thin nose, drew them in again, and walked slowly out of the room.

2

The noon heat permeated the classroom. Whispering filled the aisles. Julie said, "Lale Anderson's a slut. And so is Elzie Mayerfeld." The accusation hung in the air for a moment. Then a small girl with a tiny face said that at the German front there were probably a lot of such women, women who combined sex and song. The Little One started writing.

"We've got velvet voices, too, only we're not sluts like her," added Julie.

The girl with the scar listened to the whispered voices of the other girls. They called each other by old and new nicknames, names of animals or flowers, like the horses at the racetrack. The Dog Lady had taken them to the horse races once with Colonel Count von Solingen. Last fall they had made up nicknames solely from fruits.

She didn't even have to raise her head to know who was speaking. The father of the Fast One had been hanged for belonging to the Communist Party, although his brother had managed to go from the Communist Party straight into the NSDAP. The Dog Lady told the Fast One that before the hangman had tightened the noose, her father had betrayed all of his comrades. The Round-eyed Girl had come to the Institute because of an unsettled family situation. Her grandfather had shot himself in a brothel when her grandmother had come for him; then her father shot himself, too, so that he wouldn't have to go into the army. She had big brown eyes; the teacher promised her that for Christmas she could have them changed to blue, after the German laboratories in the east finished their latest experiments.

The Round-eyed Girl stood beneath the picture of the Fuehrer and Reich's Chancellor and grinned, showing her wide-spaced white teeth: "Who do you think is waiting for her, girls?" Then she imitated the teacher's voice: "You can go on writing, girls, while I, the Dog Lady, Elzie von Mayerfeld, walk my dogs in a gentleman's company. What's the mission of women in the Third Reich, Jenny Thelen? Bed, board, and breviary, Miss Thelen."

There were a few giggles.

"You must read *Der Neue Tag* more diligently, Jenny Thelen. Have you written your essay yet on why the British are called Jews by the Aryans?"

"Aren't you writing?" Julie asked the girl with the scar.

"I've written it once already."

"What's the matter with you?"

"Nothing. It's hot."

"Don't you feel well?"

The girl with the scar again recalled the strange excitement she didn't understand, the touch of the palm and her recurring dream of becoming a woman.

The Round-eyed Girl said, "Jenny Thelen's a dummy. A distinguished dummy."

The girl with the scar went to the window. The pavement reflected the light and sent up waves of heat.

"Is he young? Or is he old?" asked the Round-eyed Girl. "Don't tell me it's a civilian in a bowler hat. Isn't it that good-looking sailor she brought on Wednesday?"

"Do they have their arms around each other or are they just walking side by side?" asked Julie.

The girl with the scar closed her eyes. Elzie Mayerfeld was walking with the NCO. An invisible breeze passed through the street. It pressed the silk against the tall woman's thighs and tousled her hair. They were walking two slender, long-legged greyhounds. She had them on long leashes with studded collars. The dogs were white. They had slim haunches, brown spots, and long fishlike muzzles. The coats of the animals shone in the hot sunlight.

Jenny Thelen held onto the window frame, ready to duck out of sight if the teacher should turn around. But she did not turn. The girl with the scar tried to assume an indifferent air, but she felt faint. She heard words and phrases and laughter behind her. One of the girls said, "She has the tails cut off all her dogs."

The girl with the scar walked back to her desk. She felt shivers in her thighs and breasts. Her place at the window was taken immediately by the Round-eyed Girl.

"They look nice together," she said, evaluating what she saw.

"Quite," said the Little One in a resigned tone.

"You don't mean to say you'd like to prance around in silks?" asked the Round-eyed Girl.

"Why not?" snapped the Little One.

Julie turned to the girl with the scar. "We can go to the river this afternoon. She'll want to stay with him after lunch. Who knows where she's taking him?"

Jenny Thelen opened her notebook in silence.

"Will you go with us?" asked Julie.

The Round-eyed Girl was returning to her desk. "Hey, guess what? The Dog Lady's got Jenny Thelen's tongue."

"To the river?" the girl with the scar repeated absently. "Well, why not?" And then she laughed, just as absently.

"It's time for the bell," said the Little One.

"What time is it?" asked the girl with the scar.

She felt her body and her head swelling. Her own voice seemed strange. Again she was aware of being wet, literally everywhere, with perspiration. The Little One commented that women who wore ankle bracelets were fast. Someone else said she'd wear rings in her nose like the Africans did, if she felt like it.

The girl with the scar felt something within her wilting like a flower in the heat. The heat opened up her pores and filled them with perspiration. A deep languor stopped motion, time, life. Someone asked why the teacher had never been married.

Everything in the classroom around her seemed to have turned white. All she could see was Elzie Mayerfeld walking beside the NCO. They were both the same height. She tried to imagine what they were talking about. She imagined the rustling of fine silk, palms that caressed like a warm breeze, relaxing and stimulating at the same time.

Once again, she felt the touch of his hand, a sensation that mingled with the scent of the magnolias on the Superintendent's house across the street.

The Round-eyed Girl was scratching her name into the desk top: Catherine Faye. Then she sat there biting her nails. At last she said, "The Dog Lady was in the castle with some general. They had a reception in the Spanish Hall. She danced with Daluege."

"But Daluege's—you know," said the Little One.

"What do you mean—he's 'you know'?"

"I mean Daluege would be more likely to dance with another man."

"The Dog Lady couldn't care less," the Round-eyed Girl declared.

"It's the same with him as with Baldur von Schirach," somebody said.

"Baldur von Schirach? Well, he has a son. Either—or."

"Some are both, either and or. One of them must have hooked him. He's very good-looking."

The Round-eyed Girl recalled how, during the latest celebration, the air force officers lined up one after the other and sang *Hei-di, hei-do, la la.* They formed a long snake, always a man holding a woman around her hips and the woman with her arm around the man's shoulders. They marched from room to room. Among the officers was the father of the biggest furniture manufacturer in Munich.

The small girl confided: "As long as I can remember, my Father pretended he loved my mother. But that didn't stop him from throwing her best French dinners at her, dishes and all, or from throwing it all into the waste basket. When the slightest thing angered him, he'd lose his temper and shout: 'Where are the meat and potatoes?' When he was very drunk, which happened about three times a week in our house, he'd slap her or throw her down or push her against the wall and yell at her: 'Witch!' "

The girl with the scar caught only the sound of the voices, a name, an echo, and nothing more. It was all blurred by the heat, transformed into the sound of a palm sliding down silk. The smell of tobacco on the sailor's breath. His words. The way he'd called her a little lamb. The Dog Lady herself had said that one woman was seldom enough for a man.

She suddenly noticed that the page in front of her was wet. This frightened her. She quickly took out her scrap of beige handkerchief and wiped the page off.

"What's the matter with you today?"

But the girl with the scar had finally begun to write. She assumed most of the girls would want to go to the river. They'd be escorted there and back. That was the rule in this place intended for the orphans of those who'd been enemies of the Reich—whenever any orphans were allowed to remain. Meant for rehabilitation, these children had been carefully selected according to Nordic racial criteria. They were girls with Aryan forebears, girls whose destinies depended on academic accomplishment and on the testimonials of all the Institute officials.

Elzie Mayerfeld was their homeroom teacher. Prior to holding this post, the Dog Lady, in the company of three trained army dogs, had served in Sobibor near Lublin in the female guard. Now, for the girls' own good, she wanted them to forget their parents.

The first one to tell them was SS Obersturmfuehrer Hagen-Tischler, the General Inspector of Education. Their parents would have wished it, he said, had they been able to accept the inevitable. They'd have realized that their daughters were fortunate, all things considered, to have a chance of being sent to one of the old families of the Reich.

But for punishment they could be sent to the camps at the front, to the "house of pleasure"—as camp followers, or *Feldhure*—in the words of one of them who'd already been sent to the east.

The girl with the scar imagined her teacher again. She saw her wearing a lace dress, being married to Hagen-Tischler in Prague, and right after the wedding, flying to Majorca. As she wrote her answers to the questions, she kept repeating to herself that the teacher was kind, experienced, and a sincere admirer of Lale Anderson. Her two English greyhounds had brown and gray patches on their haunches. They had belonged to a Jewish family that had been moved out of Prague's German Quarter in 1940.

Once, at a spring party with German air force officers, the Dog Lady had had a little too much to drink and had begun singing military songs and smashing the crystal goblets in which they'd served the champagne. Another time, it was said, she'd received roses from Mr. Sollman, who used to leave her messages; she had occasionally left them in the lounge, perhaps trying to see who was curious enough to pick them up. Indeed, that might have been precisely what she'd wanted—as if the relationship would lose some of its importance if it were not public knowledge.

According to Tanya Grab, who'd been sent to the eastern front, the Dog lady had written some of the letters and messages to herself.

The teacher listened to everything; even when she pretended to be nonchalant, she was alert and on her guard—like the best of the Germans, like the members of the NSDAP, the SS or the SA—and as she listened she dilated the nostrils of her thin, Nordic nose. Sniffing, she took in everything that was in the air. The Fuehrer had said that nature was cruel, and so she was proud that she could be equally cruel. But she wanted to appear kind. It was in her nature to make the worst out of the best and vice versa. Her penetrating gaze saw right through the girls. The word "inform" meant the same to her as the word "honor." To believe in conscience was to give free rein to a Jewish ruse. Only the defeated found it necessary to kill in self-defense. The victor was the first to kill. In a higher sense, though, one could say that the whole German Reich was fighting a war of self-defense: defending itself against the pollution of its blood. The German Reich would last for a thousand years. Elzie Mayerfeld knew and understood why.

The windows were wide open. Heat poured into the classroom as if the boundary between the inside and the outside of a furnace had been obliterated. The Little One asked the Round-eyed Girl why Tanya Grab hadn't written since she'd gone east. It was doubtful that she'd been sent to a German officer's family. For a night, maybe, someone said. To "colonize" some officer's bedroom was more likely. The bell rang, slicing across the consciousness of the girl with the scar, ripping the silence.

The sound of the bell told her what was coming and what had passed; it was like a bullet that just barely missed its target. In it there were tender layers of light and dark, of silence and noise, of words and steps—of something that couldn't be perceived from the outside.

Finally the bell stopped ringing. Everything in Jenny Thelen seemed to fester, like a wound that had never healed: What she'd had to say to Elzie Mayerfeld—"Sorry, I forgot myself," or the days when the Dog Lady called Jenny to her or when she left to spend the evening and a part

55

of the night with an officer from the SS division Wiking from the Army Group South. Or, when his fat wife was visiting in Berlin, with the Superintendent from the magnolia-covered house across the street.

It all reminded her of a man holding a knife who lets someone bend his arm until he's forced to stab himself.

"Jenny," said Julie.

"Don't worry about me."

"You're all wet."

Someone was talking about icebergs. One of the girls remembered the winter campaign and the gloves they'd donated to the *Winterhilfe*.

"You should dry off," said Julie. "Look at what you did to your notebook."

The girl with the scar slowly straightened out the crumpled page.

"You can copy off me if you want to," said Julie.

"I'll write it myself. She'd find out."

"I bet she won't even read them."

"She always reads them."

"Almost never. Just spot checks."

"I don't want to argue."

The expression on the face of the girl with the scar revealed both objection and agreement, and something unfinished, like when you get dressed to go out and then stay home. It had nothing to do with what she was writing. The heat of the sun didn't let up. Everything seemed to be coming to a standstill. For a moment she imagined that she was drinking water, and it gurgled in her stomach.

"She's got it in for us," said Julie.

"I couldn't care less."

"How much do you have left to do?"

Jenny Thelen's pen moved again, dipped into the inkwell, and then touched the paper in the notebook. Every line, every word, called up something that was darker than the dark blue ink, something that brought on another wave of shame.

"What are you thinking about?"

"About Lale Anderson," she lied.

"That's the end of the recess," said the Little One.

The second bell rang, piercing the girl with the scar like needles—needles threaded with heat and sunlight, with words and their most secret meanings, with silence.

She felt herself filling up with silence, like a balloon expanding with dense, hot air, and then rising, regardless of where it had been anchored, regardless of where it would have to land.

3

The images flashed through Jenny Thelen's mind again, as they had so many times before, images of the day that had begun like every day before it.

Images of the day that had brought her here. She'd had no idea then of what was to come: the punishments, the programs, the people with whom her new life was to begin. She didn't yet know that the Dog Lady—although she never beat them herself—derived considerable satisfaction from watching them in the bathroom, and seeing the traces of whippings on their naked buttocks.

She squinted into the sun and then closed her eyes tightly, as if the fiery disc had branded itself onto her brain.

She saw her father going to the door. Somebody was ringing the bell and someone else was pounding on the door at the same time. They'd guessed who it was. Father went quickly to open the door, and the visitor immediately struck him across the face. Father was stunned. He turned around, his eyes filled with fear and shame, as though he were embarrassed to be beaten in front of them. His face was bloody. Mother fell when they came for her, as though she thought this might be a way to defend herself.

Two men held photographs before their eyes and asked if they recognized the girl in the picture. "No," said Father. "No," said Mother.

After that day she never saw her parents again. The Dog Lady had once told her that she wasn't alone. In Germany and in the occupied countries there were many like her, many who didn't have parents, just as there were many women without husbands, husbands without wives, parents without children, and sisters without brothers.

She couldn't go to her parents' funeral because there wasn't one.

The morning of that day had begun as usual. Mother woke her up and called her to breakfast. Father was already at the table, which was spread with a clean tablecloth; he sat drinking his ersatz coffee and eating bread with strawberry jam. For the first time in her life, she had put on her mother's silk stockings. She could use Mother's things. And then the bell was ringing like crazy, and Mother was digging her fingernails into the crevices of the parquet floor.

Elzie Mayerfeld had come for her and brought her here. The first things she told her were to be tough, to learn how to forget what had been, and to start looking forward to what was coming. To learn how to adapt. A week later school began.

Her first class was with the Inspector, SS Obersturmfuehrer Hagen-Tischler, who admonished them not to underestimate an idea simply because they'd never heard of it at home. If they'd been brought up with religion, he suggested that they look there for guidance, for "proof" that it might even be a kindness for parents to die before their children.

He lectured on geography. He covered volcanoes, earthquakes, and other natural disasters. He talked about volcanic activity that began in unfathomable depths and couldn't be observed or measured beforehand, about disasters that didn't kill or destroy, and about others that wiped out all living things.

She remembered his saying that about 1500 B.C. there had been a great eruption on an island in the Aegean Sea. An enormous mountain had been thrust into the air—a mountain whose bulk measured some eighty billion cubic meters of earth and stone. Now only the tip of the rock remained above the surface of the water; it formed the center of a small island. In a matter of minutes all civilization on that island had ended.

He also described how earthquakes were caused by subterranean movements far from the place of the eruption and could be even worse than the volcanoes we know about. She remembered every word. Every word about the water changing in the wells, the terror of frightened animals, omens of the earth opening up as if waking from sleep.

At night, under the cover of darkness, she would see her mother and father in a rhythm with her breathing. Just like Elzie Mayerfeld, Hagen-Tischler said that children knew from the beginning that they would outlive their parents. He smiled, as if to say that he had made an effort to understand them and he expected the girls in turn to try to understand him.

Since then she was only able to see her mother disheveled and in pain, the way she'd seen her that last time, lying on the floor.

"You'd better make it short," said Julie.

"I'm making it short," said Jenny Thelen.

"Then why are you writing so much? Aren't fifteen lines enough?"

"I'm doing what she wants."

The stream of images was taking her away from her notebook and inkwell, away from the girls in the class, yet it seemed to be at one with the heat and the sunlight, reflected in the glare of light from the white walls, from the windows, and from the framed glass of the pictures— among them that of the Reich's Chancellor. Everything was white and sharp and penetrating: the white of the Dog Lady's skin. Her dogs. Glowing beads of perspiration. She was sliding away from the words she wrote. She inhaled the hot air.

She returned once more in her thoughts to Kralovska Street, to their old apartment in the house by the viaduct. The picture of the unknown girl was the only clue the German authorities had to track down the assassin who'd blown up the Reich's Protector, Reinhard Tristan Eugen Heydrich, at the end of May 1942.

The newspapers said that people would be praying for his recovery. For two weeks the police searched for the girl in the photograph. In the window of one of the shoe stores on Primatorska Street they displayed her briefcase, her coat, and a girl's bicycle. It turned out later that they were really looking for seven men from England who had parachuted in. But in the meantime, General of Police Heydrich died. Rewards running into the millions were offered.

She remembered the backs of the men in leather coats. When she tried to follow the people who were taking her parents away, they had slammed the door on her; the blow had split open her forehead. Later, only the reddish scar remained.

She remembered the nights in the cell at the headquarters of the Gestapo on Bredovska Street, nights when she was almost glad that her mother and father were dead.

"Were you going to say something?" asked Julie.

"No."

Mother and Father had been executed that June at the Gestapo firing range in Kobylisy.

"Are you talking to yourself?"

"What if I am? I don't owe anybody anything."

"I hope that's not what you're writing."

Before Elzie Mayerfeld had come, Jenny Thelen had been alone in the apartment. Outside an armed police patrol guarded the door. Any signal, the slightest knock, would have helped her believe that she hadn't been abandoned; but it would not come, because the city was gripped with fear. The Dog Lady told them in her second class how in the east they killed sick dogs in special chambers with gas that penetrated everything, every nook and cranny, so that there would be no accidental survivors.

There had been the anticipated sound of approaching footsteps. Then there was the first man, the one who had beaten Father and then Mother. And the second, who had said approvingly: *Richtigbrutal,* really tough. Later, she'd strained her eyes watching the doorknob in the Gestapo office at Number 20 Bredovska Street. When the Dog Lady had finally come for her, Jenny Thelen had bitten her hand.

On the stairs they hadn't met anyone from the house. Not even the concierge, the lady who was always there, eager to pass on news from London or Moscow radio. Two men had dragged Jenny Thelen into a black Mercedes and thrown her onto the leather seat. They squeezed her between them, while a policeman held her arms. Finally she'd stopped scratching and biting.

She didn't wake up until much later, in the Julius Petschek Palace. She felt eyes watching her through a secret spyhole. But it turned out that Jenny Thelen had nothing in common with the girl in the photograph.

That's how she had come to be here in the special Prague Institute for Girls of Pure Race from Non-German Territories. It was probably because of the Dog Lady. Elzie Mayerfeld had talked with the men in the leather coats. When they were coming here by car, the Dog Lady told her that she had a choice: She could stand with ninety million Germans firmly in control of Europe, or she could stand alone against them. The black Mercedes brought her here, to this worn desk, where every morning, as a prayer, they said: Today Germany is ours; tomorrow the whole world.

The army barracks were nearby. The marching soldiers would pass by often on their way to routine drills or to ceremonial reviews. They would be accompanied by Turkish bands, wearing plumes and carrying xylophones and lyres and shrill flutes. Sometimes they would only be going to the drill field, led by the sergeant, but they always took the band.

"Everything that's past is dead. Only the present and the future count," said the Dog Lady.

At first it was drilled into her incessantly: Her mother and father were no longer alive because they'd approved of the assassination. At the same time, it was also impressed upon her that she was under German protection now, and that the German authorities paid all of her expenses.

Her last sentence was short. It was in answer to the question of why individual freedom was the privilege of only a chosen few and a chimera for the many, and why suppression was not destruction, but rather its antithesis: The Reich is the whole world.

There was something about her name: Thelen. She probably had German ancestors. The Germans had been colonizing this country for a thousand years. The best people—aristocrats, knights, men with foresight—had been attracted to the German empire, much as the Poles had been drawn to Rome.

The girl with the scar walked slowly out of the classroom. When Julie asked her why she didn't want to go to the dining room, she said she wasn't hungry because of the heat.

"Give them my name and take my fruit," she said.

"Get my swimsuit ready, will you?" said Julie.

The girl with the scar lay down on the neatly made-up bed in her room. She closed her eyes. The heat was really getting to her. She could feel it again, just as on Tuesday—the touch of the man's hand. There was something she didn't understand, something she'd heard about often enough but was encountering now for the first time. Every word and every touch had layers of meaning. The air seemed to consist of hot crystals and pearls and it seemed to be inundated by the sound of Father's Italian mandolin. *O, Maria*. Father had known perhaps eight Italian love songs. She smoothed her body with her palms, imitating the teacher standing at the window. But then she heard the rattle of tanks on the cobbled pavement of Kralovska Street under the viaduct, and she saw the German camp and the soldiers who ladled soup out of the big army kitchen kettles and gave bread to children. She was thinking about the game all people played. According to the Dog Lady's rules, girls had to play it smart if they wanted to make it in the world at all. Once again she heard the NCO calling her little lamb. He'd asked if she'd go out with him. She heard herself tell him that she didn't know. He smiled and said people always knew whether they wanted to or not.

4

The afternoon sun permeated every breath of air. It was the hottest day of the summer.

Jenny Thelen joined the girls who were going swimming. That didn't surprise anyone. It wasn't the first time she'd changed her mind.

They crossed the bridge that had the columns with the golden birds with their wings spread wide. The birds were made of cast iron that had been spray-painted; they seemed to hold the bridge up over the water. The Little One was talking about the retired general who had been the Dog Lady's admirer. The Round-eyed Girl said that the general had helped the Dog Lady get the furniture she needed, allowing her to buy cheaply from the supplies of household goods taken from the "liquidated" anti-German elements (though in some quarters, their elimination was still thought to be only a possibility).

Julie called back to the girl with the scar that it wouldn't hurt if she tried to hurry up a bit. There was no sense in wasting such a fine chance to go swimming.

She realized that other people, to whom the swimming pools were closed on Saturdays, people who were walking through the streets, were alive only because they'd sensed when it was better to keep silent than to talk, and when it was better to speak than to remain silent, even if it meant going against one's conscience. The girl with the scar thought it possible that she might run into the Dog Lady and the NCO. She fell even farther behind, but at the entrance to the swimming pool the girls were waiting for her. When the group was complete, the lifeguards let them enter.

Usually all you could hear at the pool was German. There were almost four hundred thousand Germans in Prague. Some were only passing through, some served here, and some had already brought their families to occupy apartments vacated by Jews and the houses and apartments of the incarcerated and of those who had been executed. That summer there were more soldiers than ever in Prague. They lived here as if at a resort, since the exchange value of the German mark was very favorable compared with the Czech crown of the Protectorate.

"They sing well," said the Little One.

"You call that singing? Sounds more like croaking—like frogs in a pond," said Julie.

In the last few weeks there had been a lot of invalids at the pool: mildly or seriously wounded men from the army hospital, others without arms or legs, men who were blind or disfigured with scars from burns or frostbite, men without ears, noses or fingers.

They left their bandages, corsets, and artificial limbs in the dressing rooms. Though disfigured, they still looked hardy, and they would join the groups of healthy men who sang to the accompaniment of a harmonica or an accordion or maybe just someone whistling on a comb. The girl with the scar wondered if this was the reason why, for the second season now, Elzie Mayerfeld avoided the swimming pool.

The Little One said, "After the war they'll be stringing beads, weaving wreaths, and making baskets. Would you marry someone just because he was a hero?"

Near the kiosk the soldiers were celebrating someone's birthday and shouting.

They each took a long drink of beer and then began again: *Ernst ist das Leben, Ernst soll er heissen.*

The girl with the scar changed in the dressing room and then went to look for a shady spot. She tried to ignore the badly wounded soldiers and not to think about the NCO or where he might be. A few soldiers swam into the middle of the river. The logs that enclosed the authorized swimming area were walnut-colored, stained with oil and creosote; they drifted in the water, even though they were anchored with chains.

Above the swimming pool on the hill shaped like a jumping dolphin was a park. Still higher, from the flagpole of the castle, waved the banner of fulfillment—the swastika. The bronze statues of saints that had previously graced the bridge near the swimming pool had been taken to the Reich to be melted down into cannons. And no one had lifted a finger against it, thought the girl with the scar. Neither the believers nor the patriots. Why couldn't she have a bit of that detachment?

If things had turned out just a little differently, she might not have become the orphaned daughter of criminals. Not very long ago she had had parents. A thousand years ago. During some nearly forgotten age. In the same way, no one in the future would be able to imagine what it was like here and now. Had people really lived like fish in the distant past, as SS Obersturmfuehrer Hagen-Tischler had told them?

The logs undulated with the river. The heat seemed to call up silent echoes. She felt something building inside her, even though she couldn't name it. She felt the cool movement of the river.

Her head ached, and her fingers and eyelids felt swollen. The heat drained her of all her will. She watched the logs. The submerged portions were covered with green moss and slime.

She closed her eyes and thought about rocks and gorges, about ravines and caves, about deserts and seas and desiccated wastelands and people who'd died out long ago, as SS Obersturmfuehrer Hagen-Tischler had also explained. She thought about those now living who would die and nobody would know anything about them. She thought about all of these things to avoid thinking about the NCO and Elzie Mayerfeld. She looked at the iron birds, with their cheap coat of gilt, which seemed to soar over the bridge as if lifting and suspending it above the water. The iron wings of the birds were rusty underneath. Swallows had built their nests in the steel scaffolding.

She rose slowly, then quickly slid into the water and held onto a log. In the water she could dream about what had barely started on Tuesday, about what the continuation might be. The water caressed her, touching her and splashing rhythmically against the log. She remembered what Elzie Mayerfeld considered the most important physical attributes: a straight nose, blonde hair and blue eyes, a narrow waist. And an unencumbered mind. No trace of what, before the Germans came, used to be called "conscience." She closed her eyes. She slid down, submerging her head, still holding onto the log. The wood was cool, slick, firm. She felt her whole body open up to the streaming current, to the water flowing against her.

She felt the solid darkness. She began to touch herself with her free hand, and everything became darker still. When she could no longer hold her breath, she lifted her head above the water. The sun seemed to brand her once more.

She stayed in the water for a while longer, holding onto the log with one hand or the other. Then she got out and lay on the bank, a little higher up, where there weren't any planks. She used a large piece of flat slate as a pillow. A big tree covered her with its shade. She watched the changing colors of the water, the glint of sunlight, and the streaming air.

She closed her eyes without anyone noticing. She was half-asleep and half-awake, listening.

When she opened her eyes again, she saw Julie and Catherine Faye sitting next to her.

"We're still so skinny," said Julie.

"Only in swimsuits, don't you think?" asked the Round-eyed Girl.

"Just imagine what you'd look like in silks from the Dog Lady's wardrobe."

"Only if I didn't know where she got them."

"Would you like to lie here without anything on?"

"Why?"

"I did once. It's a nice feeling. Then I saw some soldiers on the bridge up there, and I started feeling ashamed."

"Only because they didn't know you?"

"Men are afraid of me," said Julie.

"Why should they be?"

"I can tell from the way they look at me. Men are animals."

"Women are animals, too, sometimes."

The girl with the scar thought about the NCO as they spoke. She felt a nervous tremor inside, as if she'd been suddenly struck with a virus. The heat, the quiet, and the water melted into the flickering of shade and sunlight that she could feel even with her eyes closed. She lay motionless. She had a feeling that the sun and the people, the voice and the river, were there and yet were nonexistent at the same time.

"The Dog Lady's already complete," said Julie. There was experience in her voice, and it made her seem older than the rest of the girls.

Once Obersturmfuehrer Hagen-Tischler had shown the Dog Lady a picture of a hundred or so Jewish women, already undressed and waiting to be shot down in front of a ditch dug thirty meters long and eight meters deep. There were eight of those pits in a row. The Dog Lady said it was disgusting.

"What do you mean by that?"

"She's a woman. But sometimes I have a feeling she's a man in a woman's shell."

"Do you feel sleepy, too, in this heat?"

Jenny Thelen was listening to their voices and to the splashing of the water. The river trembled between two strips of land. You could hear the sound of the current, the little waves lapping the sand and stones on the bank. She still had the feeling that it was all here and yet wasn't here at all, both at the same time.

"Wouldn't it be lovely if one of them drowned?" Julie asked suddenly.

The girl with the scar didn't open her eyes. She felt warmth in her cheeks and between her thighs. The air was as sweet as milk. You could hear laughter in the distance. Birds were chirping. The tree rustled with a dry sound. The sky burned.

Then Julie said, almost in a whisper, "I could never be true to any man."

"Why?"

"Tanya Grab used to tell us what the soldiers did in the east. They took out their pistols and forced girls to kneel in front of them."

"I'd bite. Even if it were the last thing I ever did."

"If you had a choice, which would you like to be, a girl or a boy?"

"I wouldn't hesitate for a minute." The answer was implied in her tone.

"I read that deep in the ocean, where life is very rare, there lives a strange fish that, when two males meet, the smaller male changes into a female." The girl with the scar lay still and the sinking afternoon sun lay heavily on her eyelids. She felt that all of this was taking place in a dream. She knew Tanya Grab had said that, out there, for every girl of pure race there were sixteen men from the SS divisions. The State took care of the children. She felt how warm her skin had become. It seemed that not only was the river moving, but also the earth, as if it were retreating with the current into some far distance. The stone on which she rested her head was hot.

Jenny Thelen felt dizzy and didn't want to open her eyes. She thought of fish cast ashore by the waves and then stranded and of how they died, leaving bloody marks in the sand and stones on the shore; and she thought of all the volcanoes that might be about to erupt.

"Why did they send Tanya Grab to the eastern front as a camp follower?"

"She didn't want to wash with the soap they used to give us before you came. Yellowish bars, like laundry soap. It came from factories near Kracòw or Lublin and then from Danzig. Tanya Grab would sniff at it, as if it really were made from human bones."

The girls fell silent.

When the girl with the scar opened her eyes, she found herself staring with the others at a soldier who was sitting apart from the rest and rubbing the peeling skin from his shins. His legs seemed to itch and he was throwing the flakes of skin into the river. A banana peel, yellow on the outside and white inside, came floating down from the direction of the army hospital.

"Look at him scratching—isn't it disgusting?" said Julie, not sounding very happy. "It makes me sick. Why doesn't someone stop him?"

"What if it's catching?" asked the Round-eyed Girl.

"It's probably scabies. I had it once. They give you a sulphur ointment," said Julie. "They shaved my head, like they did once when they found a louse in my hair."

Then they watched the Little One trying to coax some ice cream out of an officer at the kiosk, just for fun. The officer looked her over like she was a heifer at the market; he sized up her legs, inspected her eyes, arms, shoulders. The expression on the Little One's face indicated that he might be asking too much for one ice cream. The officer was licking his cone, and his tongue hung out in surprise. He told the Little One she was some character.

"I guess I don't have the training," said the Round-eyed Girl.

The girl with the scar felt something in her soul shift, like the sun dropping in its afternoon arc. Like that rare fish deep in the ocean, changing because of a bigger male into something other than what he was. The city moved invisibly and time was somehow filled. The roofs were like burnished gold. There was a tinge of copper on the trees and on the houses in the distance. The blue streak of the horizon became more pronounced. The city lay quiet, crouched like a sleeping animal. Poplar trees grew on both banks of the Moldau. Here and there was a birch, slender and white. When the streetcar rode over the bridge, the whole rusty structure shook with a sound like rapid drumbeats. Birds were singing on the hillside.

When they were on their way home, the girl with the scar still felt as if she were lying in her swimsuit with her head on the hot stone, and as if at the same time she were floating in the water, touching the wet logs with her fingertips.

5

"It's your business if you want to starve yourself," said Julie when the girl with the scar refused to go pick up her cold Saturday supper. "I mean, what's the point of fasting all day?"

"I think it's going to turn cool," said Jenny Thelen.

"You look as if you were losing your willpower or something."

"It's just the heat," the girl with the scar sighed. "I don't like hot weather."

"I prefer the heat to the cold. It doesn't last forever, only till evening at the most."

"Why did the dinosaurs die out when they were so strong?"

"If even Obersturmfuehrer Hagen-Tischler doesn't know, how should I?" asked Julie.

The Obersturmfuehrer had explained to them once that sixty million years ago the earth had witnessed an inexplicable catastrophe, probably caused by the explosion of a star somewhere in the vicinity of our solar system, and all the big creatures perished, while rats, lizards, and small creatures, which could hide in the rocks or in the rivers or seas, survived. "It's just that there were illogical and inexplicable phenomena in nature, that's all," he had said. But it was another proof of nature's cruelty, and that was why the Reich's Chancellor was right in saying that people must be cruel, too. But another time he had told them that perhaps the dinosaurs disappeared because of a change in the weather, because it got colder, the trees stopped growing and they had nothing to eat.

She remembered what he'd told them on the Fuehrer's birthday, the twentieth of April. They were all assembled in the gym, and the army band came and played excerpts from Wagner. "You must be as proud as female eagles and as strong as lionesses. You are going to live in a world of German Aryans, and you will live like Aryans. Or you will not live at all." He never spoke of the Germans who were killed; it was as if they weren't even Germans. Once he told them that a man felt real pride only when he killed. Germany was a hammer that smashed weakness.

The girl with the scar watched the birds in the sky. They were less sharply defined now against the dark stripe of horizon.

Later, alone in the dormitory, she watched the electric clock on the wall. It said half past six. A rose-colored veil seemed to be stretched across the sky. It was just a tint, rather than the first real sign of the sunset. The sky looked like the sea. She suddenly felt a light chill, a touch of distant shivers brought on by the daylong heat. She was watching the sky change—like a mother dressing her child, removing its daytime outfit and putting on pajamas.

Looking at the sky, she thought of the sea she'd never seen, of ships she'd never known, and of islands she could only imagine, enormous rocks emerging from the bottom of the sea, their peaks surfacing above the water.

She put on her red dress, leaving the jacket on the hanger for the time being and not trying on the matching belt just yet. She thought about the heat and how it seemed to swell within her, and then subside. She felt the heat ebbing, leaving behind its many echoes and layers that had collected and were now falling apart. She could hear birds chirping in the garden. During the day they'd been quiet. Now from the window the garden looked like a green abyss.

She got up after a while and stood behind the curtains. She couldn't remember exactly what it was the NCO had said to her on Tuesday; in fact, each day that passed she remembered less. She no longer thought of how the sailor had betrayed her with the Dog Lady or why Elzie Mayerfeld had taken away her NCO.

But she couldn't escape the feeling.

Green ivy climbed the walls of the Superintendent's house across the street; the magnolias were clustered below them, with their faint but discernible fragrance.

She inhaled the cool air she'd been longing for all day, but she felt no relief, only the languor brought on by the day's heat.

The swaying of the trees indicated the direction and force of the wind. Birds flew out of their hiding places in the ivy.

The Superintendent was in the garden. He was appraising tomorrow's weather and inspecting the condition of the building's facade. Every summer he did the smaller repairs himself. He took only the faintest notice of his wife hanging out some clothes in the yard. She wore a spotted black dress. She was absorbed in herself and her laundry. He tried to avoid her glance, and anyone could guess that he wished she'd be off to her sister's in Berlin so that he could freely contemplate the Dog Lady and her older wards. The Superintendent was much fatter than his wife. When he wore his Bavarian shorts with suspenders, he looked positively ridiculous. They said his wife liked to see him that way, fat and ridiculous.

In front of his wife the Superintendent found it easy to hide his interest in the Dog Lady and his penchant for her students. He liked to ask them how they felt and he taught them things that—in their inexperience—they considered indispensable and unique. He laughed when his wife teased him about courting Elzie Mayerfeld.

The magnolias were white as swan's down in the center and their edges looked as if they were tipped with blood. They seemed a little darker now, like the evening itself: the green tenderness of leaves in an aquamarine sky that was like the envelope of a letter by an unfamiliar hand to an unknown addressee. The magnolias looked like swans, mortally wounded and bleeding from their necks. The sun had wilted them. They would soon be dead.

The paleness of the sky in the east was moving westward where it met a shadow, a darker reddish band. It looked like a woman dressed for the evening. The girl with the scar was afraid she'd stand here a long time and no one would come.

She held onto the drapes and imagined herself in a soft, bright silk dress, swinging her hips and lifting her breasts, looking confidently at the man who'd asked to take her for a stroll.

Her head was reeling. Every moment was gentle, like the breeze rustling in the magnolias, like the touch of silk on skin. The sky floated over the earth in clouds of fine mist. High in the evening sky she could see the birds flying. There were lots of them. She envied the birds. But it wasn't freedom she was thinking of.

She wished the sun wouldn't set so quickly. It was as if she were trying to gain time, to extend a deadline that wasn't hers alone. In a moment she saw the first star. The whole summer she'd watched that star in its duel with the sun. It was always the first and then the brightest, as if it came out of its shell just as the day departed, and then waited for the sun to go before it began shining. The star was still pale because the waning sun was still bright. It was Venus.

It occurred to her that, like memories, stars and planets resembled those lost islands that SS Obersturmfuehrer Hagen-Tischler talked about, whole lands that had submerged with the people who had lived there.

She had memories of her mother and father and of their life on Kralovska Street before the General of the Police had been killed. And also memories of Tuesday, when, making way for the NCO in the corridor to the geography room, she hadn't been fast enough to avoid his touch.

She smoothed her dress, automatically imitating her tall teacher.

Hidden by the heavy white curtains, she looked down again at the sidewalk. The sun felt different to her now—not the way it had in the morning. Now, it warmed and protected her and offered something she'd never had before. And she thought again of the NCO, as though she'd known him a long time and he'd just left her. That might be changed, just by willing it, to the possibility that he would come again.

From the living room she could hear the sound of steps and piano music. The Dog Lady was laughing. She was telling someone that prejudice brought suffering.

This was the second Saturday that Elzie Mayerfeld had worked at teaching them the waltz. The slow Viennese music engulfed everything. Lale Anderson was singing; it was a record of *Tales from the Vienna Woods.* She could hear it clearly, even with the living room doors closed. It evoked an image of polished shoes and women's slippers on the icy gleam of parquet floors, dancers in dashing uniforms and rustling evening dresses.

6

The music drowned out Elzie Mayerfeld's voice. She was saying something about the privilege of being able to dance while the world was seething in a fire from which a tempered Germany would rise. She talked of the happy hours when the most faithful find their best opportunities. The power of her voice sometimes robbed the girl with the scar of her will. She was happy to be away from her presence now. She could barely hear what the teacher was saying: to be patient, that they weren't old enought yet not to have to wait, but they weren't as innocent as when they'd come. The blood of German men . . . the self-denial of German women . . . One, two, three. One, two, three. The satisfaction of knowing that with what they were learning they could all graduate from the Institute into a good German family, either in the old Reich or in the annexed territories, as late daughters of some officer, camp leader, party functionary or statesman—someone who either couldn't have children of his own or who'd lost them at the front or during the air raids by the

71

British and Americans. Or they could get positions in the casinos in the newly conquered German territories that were still occupied only by soldiers.

Ten minutes later the girl with the scar looked down at the sidewalk and unconsciously grabbed at the curtain. The NCO was standing on the sidewalk. She felt again precisely what she'd felt on Tuesday. Blood rushed to her head. The scar turned pale and then ruddy again. She shivered, as if all the warmth of the hot day had left her.

"Miss Thelen," a voice called from the doorway. It was the night doorman. "Is that you?"

"What is it?" she asked.

"Lambkin," said the doorman in a friendly way. "Do you like the full moon?" He glanced around the room and put his finger to his lips, signaling that they must be quiet. The girl with the scar looked toward the window and the doorman nodded.

"There's nothing like being wanted," he said. "Good evening and all the best to you. You're to go on down. The sergeant sends his regards. Everything's taken care of. We don't have to worry about a thing."

He was bound by his word of honor, he said. It wasn't hard for Jenny Thelen to guess what he meant.

"Not a word to anyone, Miss. An order's an order, you know, and a sergeant in the navy is a promising rank, if you know what I mean." And he showed her a pack of Viktoria cigarettes, as if to remind her of the riches a sergeant could provide and of all that lay farther up the ladder.

"A minute more or less doesn't matter," he added, "but you ought to be back before midnight."

She left, flushed in the face and shivering uncontrollably. The doorman closed the gate behind her. Everything she'd tried to push down, expectations both old and new, now rose to the surface. She walked behind the building toward the NCO. She was frightened by all her mixed feelings—eagerness and satisfaction and fear, prejudice and joy—alternating waves of hot and cold. She felt a wild pain in her abdomen and tried not to think about the Dog Lady and her conquests, but to surrender instead to the pleasant breeze that pressed her dress against her thighs and ruffled her hair.

7

The NCO greeted her by kissing her hand. Blushing, she gripped her poplin jacket in the other hand.

"What was your afternoon like, Miss?" he asked.

Again, his breath was sweet and tinged with the acrid smell of tobacco, but he seemed more handsome than on Tuesday.

She didn't know what she was supposed to say or what she wanted to say, or indeed what she actually did say in response. She didn't even know later, after she had come to her senses.

The sun was going down fast. They crossed to the other side of the river where the air was supple and mild, the breeze pleasantly cool, and the moon rose white like the tip of a column rising out of the dark blue depths of the sea. Birds were singing in the trees and evening was painting the city blue. The sun threw its last rays on the rose stripe of the western horizon. She was thinking of the ease with which Elzie Mayerfeld played the part of a woman.

"Did the afternoon drag for you, too?" asked the NCO.

"I didn't know if you'd come. Military men don't always keep their word." She smiled in embarrassment. Incongruously, she thought of Elzie Mayerfeld's explanation of how dogs growled at fleas.

"I'm not like the others. Or did you have someone read cards for you?"

She wondered what it was that the Dog Lady and the NCO had in common.

In a little while the sun came to rest on the green crowns of the trees and the highest spires; it had already left the river and the bridges, as if it were letting dusk fall from a high ridge to touch the lowlands and the depressions of the city. Suddenly the flame turned red and then paled like a reflection, and the city turned quiet and beautiful. Finally even the trees and spires were dark, and windows that had caught the rosy glow now lost their tinge of pink, blanching in the light of the moon.

"It's nice here," said the NCO.

"Yes."

"The sunsets here are different from the ones at sea. On the sea, night is born differently." He said he'd been in Prague a week now and not once in the whole time had he looked at a newspaper. Then he said, "The sky reminds me of a day in the North Sea. A day in the North Sea is like night in Prague. Today was really a hot one. But I hear you went swimming."

She knew immediately on what wind he'd heard that. And for no reason at all she suddenly recalled a train ride she had taken with her father and mother; she'd watched the passing scene through a frosted window. She could see the villages flying past, the military encampments, columns of soldiers, the dirty snow.

Stars were emerging in the sky like shiny buttons on a dark coat.

"It was nice on Wednesday to watch you doing your gymnastics," said the NCO. "Girls look nice in gym suits." Then, as if to impress her with his knowledge and experience, he added, "Do you know what Socrates said? That whether a man marries or remains single, he can be sure of one thing: that he will be sorry."

He smiled at her, but she couldn't find the courage to smile back.

"What do you want to talk about? Do you want to hear about the ships I've been on?"

She asked him to tell her about himself, about what he did. She could hear the constriction in her voice and the pounding of her heart, knowing she was revealing her nervousness and wishing that something she couldn't even name would relax and allow her to open up.

Then, when she realized she didn't have to talk because the NCO would do most of the talking, it occurred to her that maybe man didn't exist just to be fooled at every turn, and she smiled for no reason. The NCO returned her smile. The full moon was reflected in her eyes.

"Don't worry. You can leave everything to me. You can't get lost with me. I know every nook and alley. I know them like my own shoes, little one." Then he told her about the ships he'd served on. He named the unsinkable cruisers, *Tirpitz* and *Bismarck*. He'd painted them when they were docked. He'd also been on two fast ships, a mine sweeper and an antisubmarine vessel. Now he was glad to be back in Prague, where he'd spent a few jolly nights. He was struck by the realization that here he talked about what happened there, and there he'd talked about what happened here. He smiled at the pleasant irony of it.

"Were you born in Prague?"

"Yes," she said.

"It's a beautiful city."

"Yes."

The NCO started telling her about all the ports and seas he had been through before coming here. He said there was no better place than Prague to take a furlough. Then he added that this was the last night of his leave.

"Where have you served?" she asked.

"All over Europe."

"I've never been anywhere outside of Prague."

"I know practically the whole continent by heart." He straightened up and unconsciously thrust out his chest.

She recalled her teacher, the silk dress with the green leaves. She could see the big roses stretched across the Dog Lady's bosom. She wanted to hold back only what was pure, only what she'd felt that morning. She was concentrating on this so hard that she couldn't quite understand what the soldier was telling her. Most recently he'd served in Kiel and before that he'd been in Prague officially, at the request of someone in the upper echelon, and had served with the unit that took part in the Heydrich action.

"That's interesting. I mean, it must have been interesting for you," she said, afraid that she didn't sound as casual as she wanted to.

The NCO felt her awkwardness and took her hand. "On my honor, *cara mia*. That's how it happened. Between breakfast, lunch and supper a man's life can begin, or change, or even end. We all had the same instructions. Kripo, Schupo, Gestapo. All three departments. It really didn't go very fast, but as I look back on it, it was a success. We were put onto the right track by one of them. Their own man." The NCO smiled, waiting for her to smile back.

"What does *cara mia* mean?"

" 'My dear.' Nothing bad. It's Italian. It's like when you sing."

"Cara mia?"

"Right. We took care of them that evening at the firing range at the edge of the city, *cara mia*. I believe it's where streetcars Number 3 and Number 14 go—the quarter called Kobylisy. Well, we didn't find anything in their apartment. They kept their mouths shut, the fools. When we pressed them about whether they approved of the assassination of the General—questions we were asking the whole populace a thousand times a day, ad nauseam—they just blinked their great calves' eyes. You know, honestly, the Slavs really look like cattle half the time."

He told her what it was they were most afraid of; he doubted they'd gotten over it. He said that putting the pressure on one man in one house in one street was enough to make all the others toe the line. It helped him understand why Germany would win the war.

She didn't ask for details and the NCO didn't volunteer any. He only remarked that brave men and cowards ended up the same way, even the ones who tried to hold onto words, as if words—just because you believe in them—could halt or change the direction of the bullets. Then he said he loved the fountains of Prague, even though he wouldn't drink from them because the birds made their nests in them.

When Jenny Thelen asked what the words were that they shouted, the NCO was pleased by her interest and by the urgency and the trace of fear in her voice, as though she were afraid to hear the full answer.

'' 'Long live the republic' or 'Long live freedom,' as if they were trying to convince themselves. Some of them demanded a last request or to write a message home. One idiot was shot still swearing that a better Germany than ours would come to replace us. As if that would make dying any easier.''

"Is it true what they say, that killing is beautiful?" she asked. Her words were barely audible.

"Usually their knees begin shaking before it comes; saliva runs from the corners of their mouths. They don't look like leaders of the anti-German Resistance. They don't look as elegant as their survivors would like to believe."

Then he added, "The greater their hope, the more frightened they are. Only those who stop hoping that something will happen—that they will be pardoned, or that some miracle will take place, the firing squad will have stopped-up gun barrels or the gunpowder will be damp—only those can stop ridiculously hanging on to life."

He went on. "Only those who no longer care, and have neither fear nor hope because they've lost everything and know it, only those are dangerous. We send them off directly to hell."

In a while he laughed: *"Wie der Vogel, so das Ei."* A mean bird lays rotten eggs.

The NCO interpreted Jenny Thelen's silence as a sign of approval. He said casually, "Even obvious cowards who'd be willing to live like mice for ten, twenty, or even fifty years, finally rush to get it over with when they're faced with our iron will."

"We aren't allowed to cry," she murmured.

The girl with the scar removed her hand from his and they walked side by side, slowly, like the other couples they met—mostly soldiers and their dates. She was glad the streets were almost empty. The NCO was quiet for a while, then took her hand again.

"Am I going too fast?" he asked.

"No."

She felt a gentleness in him that hadn't been there when he'd described the Heydrich action. He tried not to hold her hand too roughly, and it occurred to her that he had a big hand, a sailor's hand. It was smooth and dry.

"Whoever loses is always wrong," the NCO said, and smiled.

"I almost believe that," said Jenny Thelen. "You must never lose."

"How do you do that—never lose?" She smiled.

"A lot of our people make the mistake of feeling sorry for the enemy, even if sometimes they're children. There were a few irresponsible individuals who weren't only sorry for the murderers of our own soldiers, but even for young Jewish and gypsy snakes."

It crossed her mind that in his smile, as in the elegant smile of the Dog Lady, there was great pride, a pride that was great enough to destroy the last vestiges of conscience. She'd shown them a bracelet she'd been given by her sister, who was a pilot in the Luftwaffe and who was later shot down over London. It was a gold bracelet and on the inside was the inscription, "Next time both." What did she mean, "The animal is too big"?

They passed a group of sailors of lower rank who saluted the NCO. He returned the salute carelessly, not even looking at them; she felt he was looking at her. She imagined him as a member of one of the three units involved in the Heydrich action.

No one in Germany was particularly fastidious when it came to the children of the enemy, thought the girl with the scar; she left her hand in the NCO's although she didn't return his squeeze but let him lead her.

The NCO went back to his story. "Whether they were silent or shouting, they couldn't get the better of us. And silence is consent. Silence means complicity and vice versa, it. . . ." He coughed, as if gaining time to finish the sentence, but he must have forgotten what he was saying, because he started over: "There's something about it in very ancient law. Well, we're certainly as smart as they were. The ancient Romans even used this trick about silence. But I wish you could have seen them. The woman on the floor, whining like a whipped bitch. The old man leaning on the kitchen sink. And not a word from either of them. In the end people like that always have weak nerves. You stomp your foot or raise your fist and their resistance is gone. The guy had lost his glasses and he stood there blinking like an owl. Maybe he was trying to give his wife courage. So silly, just wasting time; we had plenty of bullets. The whole day I couldn't get rid of the smell of meatloaf. It's really funny sometimes, Miss. Their whole apartment, the whole building, smelled of meatloaf. A sweet and sour smell of meat, pickles and dipped bread. And then—can you believe it?—we had meatloaf for supper that night. We had a Czech cook. And then we had it for lunch the next day. Well, let me tell you, you can get too much of a good thing all at once sometimes. For a year you don't even see a meatloaf and then it's on the menu three times in a row. Your nose is full of it and you wonder where all this meatloaf came from all of a sudden.''

The NCO laughed. ''I like to come back here,'' he said. ''Prague has never disappointed me. A man needs to enjoy himself sometimes. When you're a sailor you don't know what's in store for you next.''

He was looking at the pavement, at the way the pale blue and white stones made a mosaic pattern: diamonds with circles or squares in the middle. The sidewalks of Prague were like stone lace.

''As one of my friends from the *Tirpitz* used to say, 'You climb Mount Everest only once.' '' Then he smiled. ''Every one of our men should have a chance to kill at least one of them. To purify his blood, so to speak, to earn for himself a place among the purest. It's like taking a bath.''

His voice was harsh, but it was softening, mellowing in the girl's presence.

''Would you like me to walk slower?'' he asked. He was thinking about her soft and at the same time pure Aryan face, and her forehead and neck—about her nice manners and about her shyness.

Then, thinking that she'd probably like to know more of the details, for him to elaborate—the way he had about the meatloaf—he added: ''There was a lot that happened, and if you have time I'm sure I can remember most of the details. We used to give very detailed reports— they're lying around somewhere—but I can't remember everything now. Sometimes it makes my head reel,'' he said with a little smile, lifting both arms over his head in a boyish gesture. She was happy he'd let go of her hand.

''There were an awful lot of people like that, *Fraulein*. We had to put the squeeze on quite a few. But people are like bedbugs. If you allow them to, they'll suck your blood. Particularly if they disgust you or make you afraid; then they'll suck you dry. You've got to have the courage to crush them.''

Then he said, ''I don't want to be too serious. That can spoil the pleasure of a walk. I hope I'm not boring you.''

''Not at all,'' she answered.

And then he said that sometimes it took a long time before it was all over, and other times only a fraction of a second. ''But I never envy them, *Fraulein*, whether it takes half an hour or just long enough to count to three, like it does when they use electricity to puncture the skulls of cattle in the slaughterhouse.''

He knew how to command, he said, because he knew how to obey. He told her that their evening stroll through the city was just as stimulating for him as sailing the high seas, just as exciting as fighting and feeling death in your bones. Then he thought he might have overdone it; his voice mellowed and he asked her if she knew anything about the stars. When she answered no, he told her about the constellations over the North Sea.

The city was swimming in a cool, fresh breeze. The NCO inhaled deeply and exhaled slowly. He said the air tasted like honeyed wine. Some cities, he said, looked like resorts, as though their buildings were old gems. He was happy that the heat of the day had let up.

Everything he said seemed very familiar to the girl with the scar, as if she'd heard it all before.

''Every place in this city has memories for me, *cara mia*. Aren't you cold?''

''No,'' she said.

''Do you like saying no?'' the NCO smiled.

''No.''

''We can play a game: For every three no's, you have to give me one yes. All right?''

''I don't think so.''

The NCO smiled again, as if he'd just trapped her, and then he returned to what had seemed to attract her attention from the beginning. ''It took three months to paint the keel of the cruiser *Tirpitz*. Layers and layers of protective paint. Both of them—the *Tirpitz* and the *Bismarck*—are as heavy as any ship in the world. They're huge and unsinkable, like enormous floating ice floes.''

79

The evening dusk was slowly thickening. Scattered clouds appeared in the sky and the moon penetrated them sharply, as if it were looking at them through a torn curtain.

"I'm leaving tonight," said the NCO.

"For where?"

"Kiel."

"Going to sea?"

"I'm a sailor," the NCO smiled.

"The sea must be beautiful," she said, like an awestruck child.

"Wonderful," he agreed. He knew it was beautiful, even for people who'd never actually seen it. You could hear all of this in the way he said, "Wonderful." Her silence seemed to indicate admiration and questions she was afraid to ask. Perhaps it was the helplessness of asking and waiting for a reply that frightened her, but her fear of eliciting suspicion never went further than her breathing, her voice, and perhaps a certain intensity in her silence. At the same time she was afraid of measuring everything by her own experience, since that had distorted all of her life, before and after. Her silence also held surprise and a different kind of helplessness and inexperience, as well as the satisfaction of knowing that she, after all, was the one here with the NCO and not Elzie Mayerfeld, even if she had to be second. And it was pleasant to talk about the sea. She was thinking about that strange fish deep at the bottom of the ocean, and how when two males meet in the dark, the weaker and smaller one changes into a female. But she let him talk on about the loveliness of the sea. He tried hard to stick to the topic and to emphasize how beautiful the sea was.

"You can never imagine what it's like until you've seen it with your own eyes," he said.

He was using his voice to stroke her—wooing her with the images and colors of the night sea, of the sea tossed by a storm, of the sea beneath a starlit sky—and then he took her arm in his. She didn't resist. His elbow was touching her breast and he'd become quiet.

She imagined the sea as the NCO described it; she felt a pressure in her temples and visions seemed to come out of the dusk. The whole day had so heightened her expectations that they had gone beyond the possibility of fulfillment.

Her thoughts drifted back to the blue of the sky that had dissolved now into darkness, back to the alabaster pearls of heat that had vanished in the cool evening breeze after having first been strung on threads of dust, lost now in the darkness over the city. The stars were beginning to disappear into the gathering clouds. She wanted to replace Elzie Mayerfeld just this once.

"I'd like to show you the sea close up," said the NCO.

"I don't know how to swim," she admitted.

"Would you like me to teach you?"

"That'd be nice," she said.

"Do you like fish?"

"Not particularly."

"Because they're cold-blooded, don't have a soul, and can't talk?" the NCO smiled.

He pressed against her, and the girl with the scar felt his tight, muscular body and his warmth. She could feel strength emanating from him. It was the first time in her life she had felt anything like this. She was aware of his will, and of her own as well.

Suddenly it occurred to her that any answer might give her away, even if she said yes three times in a row without a single no. She also knew she could tell him exactly why it couldn't be.

And so they walked for a while in silence; it was as though she were uncovering in her mind everything the NCO couldn't have thought of, or wouldn't have thought of in the same way she did. She felt she could never do any of the things she wanted to. In the Institute they were constantly told about the generosity and magnanimity of the Reich: the Reich that had taken them to its bosom like a true mother.

"You're trembling, little one," said the NCO. "Are you cold?"

"Not very," she said. "Just a little."

"You mustn't tremble like that," he added.

"There's a cool breeze this evening. It was so hot today."

"Come closer to me."

When she didn't respond, he added that she didn't have to be afraid. She thought she could hear real concern in his voice. He had his right arm around her shoulders and he held her close. Again she felt his strength and his warmth.

"Why are you so quiet?" the NCO asked.

"Where are those big, unsinkable ships now?"

"The *Bismarck* and the *Tirpitz?* Oh, they both went down."

"War is really cruel. And not just because everyone says so."

"War has to be cruel," the NCO asserted.

"Tell me more about the sea."

"What would you like to hear, lambkin?"

"How brave you were. How you and your friend rang the bell and pounded on the door of those people and how frightened they were and how everything smelled of meatloaf."

"I don't think we rang a bell or knocked on the door; we just pushed our way in," the NCO said with a smile. "Did I tell you about my friend? He's a sergeant now, too."

"Tell me why you've never forgotten it."

"Little one, you're so romantic."

His palm closed around her shoulder and she felt his whole hand, heavy and friendly at the same time. He looked at her and in the moonlight her eyes seemed larger. Moonlight streamed through a single gap in the clouds, as if it had been poured through a blue well.

The NCO was saying that there was a barrier between a man and a woman that a man could have difficulty surmounting. He said that when a man chose a girl, he wanted to be sure that she would be a credit to him when he took her out; he didn't want to be ashamed in front of his buddies, and he didn't want to worry about her when he was away for a long time because no sailor could avoid that.

The NCO told her that the icebergs in the North Sea looked like the white rocks along the banks of the Rhine, or like mountains with tunnels in them, or like castles, and that the water around them was always quiet and turquoise-blue and as clear as a German's soul. He smiled and told her that in war, as in nature, life and death were like brother and sister. She was more conscious of his breath than of his words.

The NCO felt a trembling frailty in her. "Lambkin," he said suddenly. And then, in the same soft voice, "You really are like a little German lamb." He told her she had a pretty face and small, feminine shoulders. And he said that he liked the way she held herself as straight as a candle, and that if she'd been born a man she'd have made a fine-looking soldier. And then he mentioned how clean she was.

She understood what was coming long before his voice broke and he told her that she looked like a lamb and that he'd never met a prettier girl. She understood it all before the first words passed his lips. Her whole life had been made up of lies; they were lies even when they were true, because everything began and ended with lies.

She started trembling as the sailor pressed her to him, repeating that she was like a little lamb. She let him lead her, obedient and docile, as though she were afraid to speak.

"You mustn't tremble like that," the NCO repeated. "Why are you trembling so?" And then he asked her point-blank, softly and rather gently, "Were you ever with a man?" There was a trace of hoarseness in his voice.

"No," she answered.

The lights of the city were drowning in a blackout. They were startled by the sound of a passing car, its lights covered with black cloth, and then they heard a streetcar that they couldn't see.

"It was so hot all day and now I feel almost cold," she said.

What did he want from her? What did he expect for a few sweet words and a *"cara mia"*? And what was she prepared to give him? She'd known for a long time that for every wrong there were a thousand and one explanations. Her father at the kitchen sink, collapsed in shame, her mother on the floor, and the whiz of a dog leash in the air.

Sometimes you wanted to forget so you wouldn't feel like a walking cemetery. But you couldn't, and the memories stayed inside of you for as long as you moved and felt and thought. You'd hear the sound of a mandolin somewhere, or you'd see a strange face with nickel-rimmed glasses and you noticed the likeness and it frightened you; or you'd recognize something in the chance sighting of a tree, a stone, or a star. Or you'd hear it in someone else's voice. You couldn't get rid of it as long as you lived.

According to Julie, people eventually stopped caring about where the soap they used came from when they couldn't get any other. She trembled at her own thoughts. She tried again to imagine the enormous ships, the freighters and cruisers. Were they like the steamboats with paddle wheels that used to run up and down the Moldau? Once her family took a ride on one of those boats—she, her father and mother, and their neighbor and his three daughters.

"A craftsman's girl would have it pretty good after the war," the NCO added to something she must have missed. "A trade is a handful of gold, as they say, *Fraulein*. If I had the opportunity, I could be a driver; I know quite a bit about car engines. And I could do quite well as a painter. Lately I've been thinking that the war will be over sometime and I ought to start looking around."

She didn't know how to respond, and the NCO added, "Of course, this isn't exactly the best time for serious commitments or marriage."

Then, as though reprimanding himself, he said, "I should try to warm you up somehow. What would you say to some tea with rum or a pastry?"

"Please," she said. "I don't want to trouble you."

"Oh, my little lady," he assured her kindly. "There's a nice place right here. Shall we go in?"

It was a self-service cafe near the viaduct. Close by were the slaughterhouse and the electric company and beyond the viaduct was the park. A freight train loaded with tanks and cannons rattled over the viaduct as the NCO led her inside.

The cafe was full of people and noise. The NCO wanted to order grog for both of them, but they didn't have rum, so he ordered a beer for himself and a Japanese tea for her. He made a point of asking specifically for green Japanese tea; he said it was as sweet as honey and good for the vocal cords.

He asked somebody at the next table for a light and began to talk quite loudly.

People were beginning to stare at them. She raised her cup and swallowed, almost choking in her haste.

She was happy when they were outside on the sidewalk again. He was saying that whatever is German is beautiful, and how difficult it is to describe it; you can only feel it. And how easy it is to recognize what is non-German. He laughed.

"Can I go back inside for a minute?" she asked. The NCO was putting his money away in his pocket and he looked up in surprise. "I need to go in by myself. Just for a minute."

He gave her a friendly smile and saw her lower her eyes and blush.

"I'll be right back," she said again.

He saw how shy she was. He smiled again. "We've got lots of time, my silly. A few minutes won't make any difference." She hesitated, and it occurred to him that maybe she was afraid he wouldn't be there when she came back.

Once she was back inside the cafe, she began to feel flashes of hot and cold; her teeth were chattering and she tried to tighten her lips. She thought of what Elzie Mayerfeld had said about living in the present, about remembering and forgetting, and about how now was always different from a while ago, as the future would be different from the present. She remembered what the NCO had said about the loser always being wrong, at least in the eyes of the victor. And she thought about his strong, warm body and his big hands and how willing he'd been to pay for her just a moment ago.

Although she couldn't stop shaking, she felt a calm deep within herself. She thought of the NCO's powerful body, recalled the touch of his hands and the sound of his voice, which was rough when he talked about the ships and about what he'd done during the war, and soft when he called her a little German lamb, and different still when he talked about what he might do after the war.

She tried to force herself not to tremble. She felt feverish after this long day. She tried to concentrate by remembering one of her mother's dresses, but she couldn't quite recall it.

Again she felt a cramp in her stomach. She was recalling the way he'd touched her on Tuesday, the feel of his heavy hand when he'd guided her in here a little while ago—all in an attempt to shake off the chill. She felt as if she were two people.

She inhaled the odors of the cafe, of the people and the food. She saw her reflection in the mirror, and the slightness of her bust surprised her. She addressed herself in her mind, scolding. The trembling in her stomach and thighs must stop.

Slowly she walked between the tables and chairs. She crossed the space between the last rows of tables and, without anyone's noticing, opened the door to the kitchen.

The dishwasher couldn't see her; she was facing the sink with her back to Jenny. Behind the cook there was a long board with several knives on it. Both women had their backs turned and were completely caught up in their noisy work.

The girl with the scar took a knife from the board and hid it under the jacket she was carrying over her arm. Her newly acquired skill at sleight of hand didn't even surprise her. It took only a second. Then she passed through a hall to the restrooms. The cook and the woman in the red rubber apron didn't notice anything.

Behind her she could hear the sound of running water and the sharp clink of porcelain. She entered the toilet stall and locked it. First she slipped the knife into her camisole, but then she changed her mind and tied it with her belt to the outside of her left thigh. She lowered her skirt as far as possible and tried moving to see if the knife would show. She remembered the NCO's saying that Prague was a capital city without fortifications. In the buttoned pocket of her jacket her ten marks lay untouched.

As she moved down the sidewalk next to the sailor, she was aware of the knife touching her body: it felt quite large, and that gave her a feeling of satisfaction. She had only to take slightly smaller steps. But she could still hold herself upright and she just had to check once to see whether the knife was held in place tightly enough.

"Here's the park," the NCO said. He'd been smoking and his breath smelled of tobacco. "I'm afraid it may rain. But the trees will protect us."

"It's awfully dark," she said.

"Are you afraid of shadows?"

He had the pleasant suspicion that she'd been preparing herself for him, the suspicion that deceives men as often as not. A man's desire, he thought, was different, simpler, than the desire or consent of a woman. And so he said, "We don't have to hurry."

He laughed without explanation. What he was saying was not really what he wanted to say, but he comforted her again. "You can trust me completely, *cara mia.*"

He led her farther into the park; his arm encircled her waist. She was afraid he'd feel the handle of the knife.

The NCO thought that in any situation a man could overwhelm a woman with images of the sea and islands, life and death, with a promise. Once more he laughed for no reason. Several times he called her "little lamb" and "lambkin" and "little one," and again he said it would be too bad if the rain spoiled things for them after such a long, hot day.

The park gate was made of wrought iron and had knockers with iron rings that were rusted from disuse. Inside the park, the air was saturated with the smell of the invisible river.

The NCO led her silently and carefully so she wouldn't stumble. She felt his hands as he touched her: her shoulders, her arms, her hips.

"It's really a beautiful evening," he said.

"Yes," she answered.

"Don't you agree that in the end everyone gets what he deserves?"

When she didn't answer, he added, "The soldier gets his moment of peace, the hungry man gets something to eat, and the lonely man gets a pretty girl."

"I don't know."

"In this darkness I can't see you unless you're very close." His voice broke again, somewhere between a full voice and a whisper, and he said, "Little lamb. My little lamb."

Then he held her close. "I'd like to ask you something. May I?"

"Why not?"

"I'd like this to be our evening."

"What do you mean?"

"Have you ever been kissed . . . by a man?" And then he interrupted himself. "Say yes, will you?"

"To what?"

"Just say yes."

"But to what?"

"Just say yes and then I'll tell you."

"No," she said slowly.

"That's enough," the NCO said softly. He said love was like a little death but he wouldn't know how to begin to explain it.

"You agree then?"

"To what?"

"May I kiss you?"

But before he could, she pulled back and asked, "Are you close to our teacher?"

The NCO hesitated. "Elzie Mayerfeld?"

She nodded.

"Oh, you lambkin. Elzie Mayerfeld is a distant relative, a fifth cousin or something. Our cow drank from their trough, as they say. She thinks I left hours ago. Why do you ask? Oh, yes. You'd better not tell her anything. Girls sometimes like to boast."

She said he didn't have to worry about her telling anyone. The NCO smiled at that; he was trying to find a properly secluded place for them. He held her so tightly that it frightened her; he misinterpreted her fear.

She could feel his hot breath and his strong hand. Then he was leaning over her, whispering, "Would you like me to be close to you?" His whisper was more penetrating and insistent than before.

"I don't know," she whispered back.

He led her away from the walk, over the grass and into some shrubbery. The ground was damp and crumbly, wet with the evening dew. She seemed to him compliant and soft, excited by the nearness and the increasing intimacy of a man who could no longer be refused. He knew that was why she was trembling. Her lips were pressed tightly together, which he interpreted as the anxiety of inexperience.

Her heart was pounding. And she could hear another pounding mixed with the sound of her heart.

She watched the NCO while he kissed her, and she saw images of other men in uniforms and leather coats, as if the many had become one, and each individual contained the first and the thousandth.

"It will be beautiful," the NCO whispered. "You'll see. It will be just like I promised." He caressed her with his palms and his fingertips, touching her cheeks and around her lips and then brushing his fingers over her forehead and stroking her scar.

She let him do it. She felt blood rushing to her cheeks. She was thinking of blood, terrified of what she could see in her imagination.

"Did they hurt you?" he asked. Then he added hoarsely: "I won't let anyone hurt you. No one will ever hurt you again."

With both hands he caressed her cheeks, and her shoulders, and finally her breasts. She knew what was coming and she was afraid he might find the knife.

"We're alone here," the NCO whispered. "I don't want anything bad. Only something we can have together, now, right now. Something we can remember. Nothing that would hurt you. You're lovely. You're so lovely . . . We should seize life while we're still young . . . a few stolen moments once or twice a year . . . don't think about anything . . . ugly . . . come closer . . . let me . . . lambkin." His voice was getting more and more hoarse.

The girl with the scar pulled back a bit. He thought she was merely confused by his whispered words, his caressing palms, his breath.

"No one's here," he whispered again. "The local people aren't allowed here in the evening. No one will disturb us here."

"Yes," she whispered. "Yes. But turn around for a second. Just for a second."

"Why? What's wrong?" he asked in surprise.

"I have to fix something."

The NCO heard her untie her belt; then he thought he heard the unmistakable rustle of a lifted skirt and the scratch of a fingernail against naked skin. He coughed in his effort to suppress an impulse to turn abruptly, take her in both arms and pull her down onto the grass. The blood was rising to his head. He imagined that her skirt was already off. He gave her time to take off her blouse and unfasten her underwear. It began to rain softly.

THE GIRL WITH THE SCAR

"OK?" he asked.

"Not yet," she whispered.

She had taken out the knife. Compared with the NCO she was small and weak; she'd have to give it a good swing, as far back as she could and then forward. She felt such excitement that she couldn't think of anything beyond the stabbing. She felt the pain in her abdomen, but she didn't allow herself to think about it. There was only a fraction of a second when she was paralyzed by a strange anxiety about the success of what she was about to do, like someone who had never killed before, but had lived, breathed, and grown up in the midst of killing. The anxiety left her as soon as she moved the arm with the knife, and so did any tremor that might have weakened her. She felt the point and then the wide blade enter his body silently, with almost unbelievable ease. She had struck him lower than she'd intended, and because the NCO had started to turn around, she'd struck him in the area of the kidneys. Then the movement of his body caused the knife to twist in the wound—as she held onto the handle—with a convulsive force that in only a moment began to ebb.

The NCO groaned hoarsely, as if he were trying to exhale without having drawn in a breath. The insistence of the sound was familiar to her. No final cry came from his breast. He was falling slowly, as if he were only lying down. As he fell, his body parted the thick bushes in front of him. The bushes opened with a plaintive, broken, rustling sound, and then closed over him again.

The NCO's hand grasped the knife, but he no longer had the strength to pull it out. He choked a little longer. The rain was soft and warm. The park was full of birds; they were roosting everywhere, on the ground, in the trees, in the bushes.

The girl with the scar straightened herself and walked out of the shrubbery onto the park road. She met no one on the way to the gate. The local people were forbidden to use the park, and anyway, no one would have wanted to come here in the rain. It seemed to her that she was strangely calm, as if she were divided in two. One was quietly walking, obediently trying to forget voices and faces, as she was daily advised by Elzie Mayerfeld. Inside was the other: She had lived with her a long time before getting to know her. Now at last she could recall her mother's wedding dress exactly. Her mother used to take it out at least once a year; she would shake out the wrinkles and air it before putting it away again.

Her father was walking with her, too, his nickel-rimmed glasses on the bridge of his nose. He looked like a professor, even thought he'd worked for years at the waterworks. He played the mandolin and sang *O Maria*. He told her that the tall trees bent with the wind and that the low trees could withstand storms precisely because they weren't so tall. And what a pity, he said, that the magnolia blossoms died so soon. She was telling him not to be afraid.

8

Drenched to the bone, the pale girl with the scar walked through the front hallway of the Prague Institute for Girls of Pure Race from Non-German Territories. Her belted poplin skirt and jacket hadn't protected her much from the rain.

"Home already?" asked the doorman. He was reading *Ost Front,* his face a mask of cordiality. "Lambs always seem to suffer from a lack of four walls and a roof over their heads," he said. "But if you can't do it under the open sky, you shouldn't do it at all."

"He left," said the girl with the scar. "For Kiel." She gave the doorman her ten marks. He quickly stuffed them into his pocket so they wouldn't get wet.

"Too bad," said the doorman, as if asking whether it didn't hurt. He smiled like a man who could draw his own conclusions. He was showing off his second pack of Viktoria cigarettes. "That's the way to do it, Miss. You have to elbow your way up in this world. We can't be like the English who missed the boat. That shouldn't happen to us in this dump." And then he added, "We must all answer for every opportunity we get, don't you think?" He was closing the gate behind her. "On my word of honor," he said slyly. "One good turn deserves another. Not a word. Not to a soul, ever." He raised his thick black eyebrows.

Upstairs in her room the girl with the scar untied her belt. There wasn't a trace of blood anywhere. All she could feel was the pulsing of her scar. She remembered the goldish bronze urn they'd shown her in Bredovska Street. The warm calmness within her did not leave. They were still dancing in the living room.

She put her jacket on the chair, then took off her red dress. She took out her comb and began to comb her hair. In her small bosom, which was quietly heaving up and down, there was no trace of what she'd feared. Nor did she cry. Next door, the record player was playing Johann Strauss's *Tales from the Vienna Woods*. The voice of Lale Anderson was velvety soft, and the melody was like an open embrace or a couple's joined hands.

In the darkness she thought of the soaked, softened earth, of the voices of birds waking at sunrise, and of worms, of earth and light. She imagined the magnolias opposite the window, blossoms whose centers were as wet and white as the throats of swans and whose edges seemed dipped in blood. Inside herself she was talking with her father and mother; the dead were the only ones she could talk to. Only the dead could be told the truth.

She combed her hair slowly with the easy, languid movements of a woman. She saw a white darkness in which she could imagine blood, perhaps spilled by a she-wolf biting through the neck of its mortal enemy.

She wanted to grasp the change in herself. But she couldn't. She felt her life was part of the rain, like a river or the sea. She knew she had done what she had to do to fulfill the secret purpose that existed in everyone's life.

She opened her eyes. Images of streaming water turned back into the furnishings of her room: the wardrobe, the desk, the bed on which she was sitting. The comb she combed her hair with. The waltz music filled the house, the garden and the night.

She took out some dry underwear and a clean dress and threw all that she'd taken off into the waste basket.

The belt lay on the floor.

Indecent Dreams

1

THE old woman's complexion was like the bark of a tree. She walked up to the cinema box office and handed two tin pots of food through the window. The cashier slid the long book of tickets for the next day's program to one side. "Thanks," she said.

"You're welcome," said the old woman. "You know how glad I am to be able to do this for you, honey. It's potato soup and in the other pot there's lentils and smoked meat."

The building was old and occupied a whole city block, like a palace. Italian masons had been brought here at the beginning of the century to build it. One of the owners had converted the former concert hall on the ground floor into a cinema. The middle floor, which had served as the owner's residence until he sold the building and moved to America just before the war, was now a courtroom. The basement, for reasons no one understood, was a dormitory where railway men from the three main Prague railway stations slept. A cloakroom with showers, a dining room, and bedrooms were located in a former massage parlor that had been forced to close when the owner failed to pay the rent.

Most of the verdicts handed down by the German judges in Prague in the spring of 1945, the last year of the war, were simplified to either life in prison or the ax. But the cinema below continued to show German operettas as it had before (except for five days when a state of mourning for a German defeat on the Volga was declared throughout Germany and even the occupied territories), and the theater was usually full, even during morning and early afternoon matinee performances, not to mention the evenings, when it was practically impossible to get tickets just before the film began.

The cashier was young and pretty, with fine features, perhaps a little melancholy even though nothing had happened to her during the war. Her fair, magnificently combed hair fell to her shoulders and her blue eyes never lost their ingenuousness, not even when she took a large banknote from a customer and carefully returned the proper change, concentrating fully on her job even though she was sometimes genuinely exhausted. The prettiest thing about her was her long neck: sometimes it looked like that of a purebred race horse.

"How are you, my darling little girl?" asked the mother.

"I've got some kind of rash on my neck," replied the cashier.

"Does it hurt?"

"No, it just itches."

It was the only animal-like thing about her, even though the animal it called to mind was beautiful. Perhaps not even that was just, because at the same time her neck was like that of a white swan. Something about her suggested loneliness, though her mother, with skin as wrinkled as an old tree, was never far away; and even now when she had a job, her mother never left her alone for very long. She would walk her to work every day from the working-class suburb where the most imposing structure was a huge round silver natural gas storage tank supported on tall sturdy steel lags. Together they would walk from the tangled labyrinth of small, ramshackle houses, some made of wood, others with stone or half-stone walls. There were no paved streets and they had to wear galoshes to avoid getting covered with mud before they reached the center of the city. To the old woman, her daughter meant everything that was valuable in life. She begrudged her daughter nothing, not even her fine clothes, in which the young woman looked above her station. Everything about the daughter suggested she was a person who knew how to look after herself well.

"I'm almost glad you never married," said the old woman through the window. For a moment her face relaxed. "I'm happy you're going to come out of this pure, not like those tramps who hang around with any rank at all—colonels, lieutenants, even privates," the mother added.

But her mind was full of thoughts she didn't confide to her daughter: There are a lot of young men hanging about with those vests made of rabbitskin turned inside out. Where have they come from? What are they looking for in the center of Prague? They all look like bums. You can't believe anyone. Perhaps the mother was genuinely glad that her daughter was still single, but it wasn't so certain the daughter shared her feelings, even though she didn't look unhappy.

The cashier sensed what her mother was thinking. The mother didn't trust people—people on the street or in the elevators of tall buildings where she occasionally went on errands for her daughter. Sometimes she was afraid even in the corridor of her own building before turning the key to unlock the door of her own flat.

"Will you wait till I finish eating?" asked the cashier.

"Some places they've already started taking German signs off the buildings," replied the mother. "Some of the trams have removed their route signs. And I'll bet it's not just so the Germans won't know where they're going." And her eyes said: There's something in the air. Something's about to happen, I can feel it in my bones, my little girl. We have to be careful.

"What's playing?" the old woman asked.

And she wondered why a person always felt threatened by something, like spring comes before summer and like summer comes before autumn takes its place, and like the wind and the rain come, or like the sun and the snow. A strange yet familiar anxiety came over the old woman, a feeling she'd never get used to, not even if she were to live a thousand years, and sometimes she felt as though she had been in the world a thousand years already, though she was scarcely sixty. Fear, thought the old woman. She sometimes trembled for no reason at all. As though fear had accumulated within her, not only fear for her own life, but for the lives of her mother and father, the parents of whole clans stretching far into the unknown, where only the rich or the famous are concerned for their destiny. What was she to them?

She looked at her daughter—at her swanlike neck, at her frank, somewhat timid eyes in which there was a light, dreamy haze, and she longed to penetrate her daughter's thoughts where unknown films were shown, different pictures. The old woman was afraid of the men who were interested in her daughter without her knowing about it. It wasn't just the Nazis who reserved the right to steal, kill, and lie. The poor thing has pimples just like a woman who needs a man; but she didn't trust her with anyone, not for anything. You have to be as clever as a fox, my little girl, strong as a tiger, and changeable as a chameleon. Not give yourself over.

What kind of storm would come bursting forth from the clouds hanging over the city, as though night were falling everywhere? She couldn't see properly. I don't like it when it gets dark. I don't like it when the day ends, when something is coming to an end. And no one knows anything, thought the mother. This is that unknown day, when no one knows anything, when everything can be first or last, last or first.

"Still the film about the two sisters," replied the cashier. "It's intermission just now. Do you want me to buy you some ice cream?"

"No, no, it's just made from water and artificial sugar anyway. Don't bother, darling."

Her mother's "no" was like an explosive tossed into the air to destroy something else. At least once a day, she said the more you trust people, the sooner they'll cheat you. The less you trust them, the better.

"You don't have any dish powder," she said finally. "Give me the dishes, I'll take them back."

What's the matter with me? she asked herself, because she could see the same question in her daughter's eyes. What am I really afraid of? What do I care about others? Why do I tremble when nothing is happening to me? That's how it's been for six whole years, she thought. Perhaps I'm just blaming it all on the Germans. I was afraid even before. But no. It's like the eclipse of the sun the newspapers are predicting for next week.

"I've never liked this building very much. Everything is too big. I've never been very fond of your cinema, either. The Morgenstern where I used to take you when you were a child was nicer. And I don't even like most of the programs."

"I'm glad I have a decent job," said the daughter.

"A decent job? Yes, at least you've got that," admitted the mother.

"It's warm in here."

"And it's not dangerous, that's the main thing, little girl."

"Remember that lanky guy, the one who moved out of our neighborhood and used to come here for sausages? He was just here looking for his brother. You didn't happen to see him on your way over, did you?"

"The one with the big teeth? Isn't he still selling papers?"

"Yes, he says he's worried about his brother. He says his brother saw God."

And the mother thought: To buy sausages? I'll bet I know who he was coming here to see.

The cashier laughed. Everyone has different visions. She had her own secret dreams, but instead of dreaming them at night, she dreamed them during the day while counting tickets or money or while sitting alone and eating, as she was doing now. Her own indecent dreams. But she couldn't tell her mother about them. She'd faint from the shame, because they were forbidden dreams. They weren't about Germans, nor about freedom. They were about men, and she was always in them, but they went beyond the bounds of what her mother would allow. They were terrible to imagine, and they made her dizzy with fright. She'd perspire all over. And that wasn't all.

Echoes of passions, of sin and sinning, went through her head, echoes of naturalness and shame. Visions of gallant love, romantic affairs or explosions of jealousy followed by shyness, shame and secret dissatisfaction; disillusion and even hate and injured pride at some moments. It was a haze of stories she had seen at the movie theater; but it was more than that. At the bottom of a stream no one knew about, there was something she wanted so much. She thought about a woman's courage. Why it means so many different things. Sometimes she dreamed that she was a river with many tributaries, flowing and flowing but never emptying into the sea—just circumnavigating the world and then emptying back into herself again.

"No, I didn't see anyone and I don't want to. Is the owner of the cinema here?"

"I have no idea. I haven't seen him," replied the cashier.

"Better that he's not here. I don't like it when he's around," said the mother.

And she thought: Each day I'm more and more frightened for you. Each hour. Why? Has it really been like this all my miserable life? Is there nothing beautiful in life? Is there only eternal, endless fear? Why does everything seem alien? I can see right into the owner's stomach. All I have to do is think of him and the feeling comes back. The richest people think the whole world is there to serve them. They're all the same, she said to herself.

"He's very polite to me," said the girl.

"Can you trust his politeness?"

"Why not?"

"Don't forget he once pestered you in a very nasty way," said the mother, and again she thought: He has eyes like a toad. I've never seen uglier eyes. He looked at your breasts so shamelessly, as though he were admiring you, but he envied you your beautiful breasts. Men envy a lot about women. I know men like that, I know what they want. White flesh, innocence, tenderness. The things I've had to do for them when they paid for it. The more money people have, the surer they are of themselves. They think they can do everything. You need a strong stomach. They think a girl will swallow anything, literally anything.

"Don't worry," said the cashier. "Come on inside. Why are you always afraid? What good does it do you?" She smiled. She had white, regular teeth. Her mother had taken great care to see she never needed a filling. "You end up being afraid to breathe."

He could charm you, thought the mother. She watched her daughter as she ate. And where would you get the money for decent cures? she thought.

"For years now we haven't been able to lead a normal life," she said out loud. "That's what it is." And she added to herself: People take great delight in murdering each other. They always have. People are animals, that's why they kill each other. There are only a few exceptions, people who respect themselves, like you, my little girl. Like me. The Bible says we were all created in the image of God, but only from the waist up. Open your beautiful blue eyes, my sweetheart, so you'll see all the shadows that follow you around. Hitler and Mussolini and Kaltenbrunner and Mr. Karl Hermann Frank. I could go on forever. The world has gone mad and we must try to go through it untouched, my sweet child. That's why we live inside ourselves, my darling, and everything that goes on outside doesn't require us for its doing. The world may be beautiful and yet it is terribly bad. No one loves anyone for long. That's why so many commit suicide, my darling.

"What are you thinking about?" asked the girl.

"Don't ask."

When have I ever not been afraid of something, can you tell me that? Only when I gave you my breasts and my milk. Then I felt the world was at peace. My breasts were firm and pliant. I was filled with love. But as soon as I finished feeding you, I was afraid again. And again it's in the air. The murdering will begin, child. It's here. Some things are beautiful only when you're young. Even though people try to persuade themselves that wisdom comes with age, it doesn't. The heart grows cold, that's all. I know what it means to have a broken heart. And I know what will break it: a long life. Waiting. Fear. Hopes. Lies. The truth, my darling. The naked truth.

The mother sat on a box containing old posters. She looked at her daughter as though she were expecting her to lay an egg.

"Why don't you rest here a while and then go home and lie down," said the cashier.

"Why should I rest? From what?"

"You look like you have a fever."

"Why aren't you eating, my child? I made it hot for you. You're letting it get too cold."

"Do you think this is the day we've been waiting for?" asked the cashier suddenly.

She didn't finish her food. Her mother always gave her more than enough, as though she didn't believe she'd be able to eat again the next day. She put the lid back on the pot and fixed it in place with a strong elastic band. She wiped the spoon off with a dish towel that hung on a peg. The towel covered a poster displaying the face of the German actor Heinz Rühman. The second pot had contained the potato soup, but the cashier had finished that.

"People are like animals," said the mother.

"People never get tired of enjoying themselves," said the cashier.

"Are you always sold out?"

"Pretty much."

"Something's about to happen," said the mother. "But you mustn't get mixed up in anything. You've never done anything to anyone and I don't want anyone to do anything to you."

"You said the same thing last year."

"It's in the air. Last year, this year, right now."

"Maybe."

"Someone said the staff of the British Embassy has moved up just outside of Prague." The mother watched her daughter, studying her mouth when she talked, her eyes when she looked at her. What do you know about debauchery? she thought. Luckily for you, you've never had to go through what I did.

"And the Germans pretend they don't see anything," added the mother. "As though Prague were an island of tranquility. An open city, as they say. A hospital city where they send the wounded to recuperate." The mother began to whisper. "As though they'd all forgotten, as though no one remembered anything, just because the Germans are getting beaten and their leader isn't recruiting fourteen-year-old boys anymore because he's dead and those who took over from him are urging them on and giving them rifles. And they still go to the movies and think that operettas will get them out of their fix."

The Germans are like rich people, thought the mother. They think they can do anything they want, not just kill, lie, and loot. When people think they can get away with it, they'll do things they ordinarily wouldn't dare.

"They'll be sorry once it starts," said the mother quietly. She had to wipe saliva from her lips. When her daughter was small, the mother thought, you could still believe that everyone was born the same, even though people are never the same, but they weren't worse just because they were different. The Germans beat that notion out of people's heads and now people are going to start beating it out of the Germans' heads. "That unknown day. That long-awaited day." Even those who are different will end up killing each other.

The mother shuddered and stroked her daughter's elbow. The girl had long arms and fingers, and supple skin. The mother thought: You might have played the piano beautifully, my child. That day. A mockery of anyone who has made himself at home here for six years with a pistol, a riding crop or a cane, carrying on with the local whores and beating up anyone he felt like.

On the street in front of the building that housed the cinema, an elderly German soldier with a raw, chafed neck appeared. He looked into the box office.

"He's in fine shape," whispered the mother.

"They'll be singing a different tune soon," said the daughter.

"Where do you suppose he came from?"

The man's neck looked as though they'd tried to hang him and the rope had broken. He shuffled over to the sausage stand and ordered a frankfurter. Then a second soldier appeared.

The second soldier ordered two tickets and paid in marks. Now it was obvious that a colleague was waiting for him a few steps from the box office. Both of them looked at the girl with appreciation.

"It's a fine building," said the first.

"Sure, but the cinema isn't the best thing about it," replied the other, and he laughed through a set of rotten teeth. "The teller's desk, the little nest." It was rather a nice laugh.

"I think I'd better wait for you," said the mother.

"No one will try anything," said the daughter. "They're just looking. They've probably had no company for a long time."

"On my way here, people were scraping the letters off German signs. They were standing on chairs, stepladders, and tables so they could reach the ones that were up high. There was a crowd on Charles Square."

And then she said, "One man there—it was near the Black Tower—was shouting that every soldier killed this Friday night by our people will make up for one of ours killed by them. I thought I recognized him. It was one of those two, you know who I mean? Both of them are tall and lanky."

"Were the police there?"

"No."

"Why didn't you tell me right away?"

"I wanted you to eat first. I put a spoonful of bacon fat in there for you. It's good for your complexion, child. I saw some young fellows in rabbitskin vests beating up a Hitler Youth kid. And there was a man shouting that they were doing it for Sonitschka Vagnerova. He looked a bit like the brother of that long-legs."

"I wouldn't be surprised if it was," said the cashier. She was upset that her mother hadn't mentioned it right away.

"Are things quiet here?"

"My boss told me crowds were gathering. He told me I could sleep in the cloakroom if I wanted."

Her mother never told her anything, not even how much money she had in her savings account.

"I hope you turned him down."

That's just what he wants, thought the old woman. A nice piece of young flesh in the cloakroom. He'd certainly filled his pockets during the war, and all because people wanted to forget (however briefly) and were willing to pay for amusement.

"I hope his ardor cools," the mother added. And she thought: Perhaps this is the day. How many times have I imagined it to myself? The owner certainly would love to have a nibble, that's for sure.

And she said to her daughter: "It's an odd thing in itself when the police are polite."

"Can you wait here for me?" the cashier asked. "Those were the last tickets. We're sold out now, both the balcony and the orchestra. The soldiers don't care if the film's half over. I'm going to hand the money over to the boss."

"All right, my sweetheart, but can you lock me in here? And don't be long."

The girl closed the window and the door. The mother stayed behind and thought: I don't want to remain alone. I know what it means to be alone. I know what loneliness is, my little chicken. It's like a cramp. It's like a splitting headache. It's that unknown day. That unknown day, the one you think will make up for everything, if only there's some meaning in it. What will that day hold? What will it have to hold? She knew herself what it would hold, apart from the mothers who lost their children and the children who lost their mothers and fathers, brothers who lost sisters, and sisters, their brothers. How many fathers had betrayed their own grandmothers because they feared the authorities might prove she had a drop of Jewish blood in her? How many people had been disposed of simply to accommodate the Germans? And then there was the personal aspect. The most personal thing of all, something that you'd never betray to anyone.

The old woman in her black widow's dress sat on a crate of posters in the box office and waited for her trembling to stop.

2

The cashier stood beside the tall fellow's brother. She looked at the German automatic pistol jammed deep into his belt, so that only the handle stuck out. The rest was hidden by his buttoned jacket. She went to turn the money over to the owner and when she came back, she looked down the passageway into the street at the sausage seller and the sweetshop opposite.

"How is your dog doing?" she asked.

"Law? I left him at home."

"Why didn't you take him along?"

"He's sick. I don't want them to shoot him."

The lanky fellow's brother smiled, showing his few teeth. He'd named his three-year-old Irish setter just after the assassination of the German secret police general, Heydrich, at the end of May 1942. A German truck, driven by a drunk driver, ran over the puppy's bitch-mother at high noon, just as it had run over a well-known Jewish poet near the National Theater earlier.

The lanky fellow's brother smiled at the cashier a little longer and smoothed out his creased and shaggy rabbitskin vest.

"How do you feel? Everything OK?" the cashier asked.

"It's OK," he answered.

"How could we have let it happen?"

"How? We were blind. Because we couldn't conceive of the horrors people just whispered about."

He thought of the dog and wondered why the animal was so faithful. He never felt quite worthy of the dog's love. It was lavish in its devotion. He believed the dog would actually die for him. Law wasn't timid. He met strangers head-on, level-eyed, never giving ground. With Law, the lanky fellow's brother's every movement was quietly observed, even when the dog was sleeping. If the young man moved, the dog's eyes would open and follow him. He could never get too far away because Law wouldn't let much distance come between them. He'd heave himself up, stretch and flop down beside him again, protective and content.

"You look pretty nice."

"Thank you. As you can see, my luck stopped there."

The cashier looked at the tall fellow's brother and thought the dog was an extension of his self-satisfaction. She liked this in the dog, but wondered why so few people had such a quality. Sometimes he was ashamed in front of his dog because he was shy and timid and held back when confronted, until he was really provoked. But then it was usually too late and he'd vent his anger alone, unlike Law, whose anger showed right at first. It was funny, she thought to herself: He could control his dog's destiny but not his own.

"What if it's too soon?" she asked the lanky fellow's brother.

"One of them dropped it," he said. "They gave him a real roughing up. I was the first to get to it."

"My mother saw you."

"I never noticed her there," he said, watching the cashier with his murky eyes.

"Your brother was here looking for you."

"I was in Bredovska Street, near that Jewish palace where the German secret police are, the Gestapo headquarters. They're ready for us. They moved tenants out of the best apartments and turned them into machine gun nests. They're armed to the teeth."

"He was with the owner here. He was looking for plans of the building. He wanted to know the layout of the basement."

"I sent him here. Maybe I missed him. I thought he would wait."

"He was a little nervous. He said you'd had a vision of God."

"That wasn't all I had a vision of, but it was the most powerful."

"What do you mean?"

"It's like a fire, spreading from person to person. I mean it, miss. It's like a disease, but it brings people together instead of tearing them apart. You don't happen to know where they buried him, do you? I never saw any mention of a funeral in the papers. Just that he died in his underground bunker. A million tons of concrete must have fallen on him. Tons of rock, granite."

"No idea."

"Did they get those plans?"

"Yes. The owner gave them to him. Your brother went away then. He was anxious to find you. He said if I saw you, you'd know where he went."

"I had a dream. We were in your theater. You sold me a box seat. She took her star off. We held hands. She was as beautiful as Venus, and as gentle as a sleeping volcano. She told me to come to the house with the marble facade after the movie was over, the house where they lived until Hitler came. She said she'd go first and get ready. Before she'd always been so standoffish. But when I wanted to touch her—I mean in the box with the red velvet—she pushed my hand away and told me not to do it and said, 'Such a muddle.' That's exactly what she said: 'Such a muddle.' Do you think I'm in my right mind?"

"I think you can probably make some sense out of it yourself," laughed the cashier.

The tall fellow's brother was wearing a vest made of uncured rabbitskin. He was talking, as he had the time before, of Sonitschka Vagnerova. They were standing at the end of the passage. Some young people wearing the same kind of vests were smashing the window of the sweetshop across the street. They took a sign that said, "No Admittance to Jews," turned it over, and one of them wrote on the back: "Long Live the Free Republic. Death to German Swine!"

"That's exactly it," said the lanky fellow's brother. "That's exactly the kind of thing they wrote about people like Sonitschka Vagnerova, except now it's the other way around." The sweetshop is going to be a wreck in a few minutes, he thought.

"I feel as if it had nothing to do with me," said the cashier, "but it's not because I don't want it to."

"I like watching it. It's as though you'd been angry with yourself for a long time and now suddenly you see you don't have to be anymore. I hope I never have the strength again to be as angry as they were."

"You should go looking for your brother so you don't miss him," said the cashier.

"Can I use the bathroom to fix myself up a bit?"

"Do you know where it is?" asked the cashier. She could hear people speaking in the railwaymen's dormitory. The courtroom overhead was probably empty.

"They're giving it to them for her, too," said the lanky fellow's brother.

"For whom?"

"For Sonitschka Vagncrova."

The cashier tried to guess what he meant. I mustn't feel jealous, she reminded herself.

"And for every one they humiliate, ridicule or beat from now on," he added. "For every one they rob of what he's worked for all his life, or deny what he has the right to. When they hold someone's mother against him, or someone else's father. And when they lie to someone, steal, and murder just because he wears glasses or is weak and sickly. They can take that swectshop apart, if they like."

"Was she that nice looking girl who spoke like a ditch digger?"

"I couldn't get her out of my mind when they were taken away. They left that house with the marble facade. They had a used car lot."

"She was a very practical person, I remember that."

"For two and a half years, ever since November 13, 1942, I've kept watching that house just in case they come back. In that booth you sold us the tickets from, I pressed up against her. More than anything else, I long for her warm white belly."

By now the sweetshop had been ransacked and they were starting to wreck it. One of the young men began to smash the chairs against each other. They were shouting. The cashier looked at the inscription they'd written on the back of the sign. My mother is right, she thought. We're all animals.

"Do you think a girl who lives in a tiled house is suitable for a boy from the slums?"

"When I look back, it seems to me now, too, like calling a dog 'miss,' but anyway."

"I hope you manage to meet up with your brother," said the cashier, almost testily.

"I can even tell you where it's supposed to be: across the river, by the tracks."

She went back to her mother. The lanky fellow's brother left, and his last words were that he'd never seen chairs broken so beautifully before. He thought about the things he'd seen in his vision, just as real to him as those kids in the fur vests ripping apart the sweetshop, and he brought his brother a pistol to show him that while one of them was getting the plans of the cellar, the other had been assembling an arsenal. He knew what his brother had told the ticket seller.

He thought about two things. The first was that from the moment the Nazi defeat was certain, the Germans had chosen to feed their own illusions.

Hitler had given orders for the German Army to be divided into a northern part under Admiral Doenitz and a southern part under Marshal Kesselring. Both were told to expect a conflict between the American and Russian armies over who would control Germany. They needed a space that could be defended until the Allies started fighting among themselves. They created what they called the Alpine National Fortress and the Bohemian Zone. There was no demarcation line in Bohemia and that could well be one of the sources of conflict.

The other thing he thought about was how he'd pressed close to Sonitschka Vagnerova in the cinema and how she'd said, "Such a muddle."

He dreamed that he'd bought underwear for Sonitschka Vagnerova, just the kind he'd heard lovers bought for their favorites. But in his dream he had only a vague notion of what kind of underwear it would be.

Thinking of such things made him feel hot, as though he were slaving away in an underground shaft somewhere in Venezuela where it was seventy degrees Celsius. That's where everyone who has a Sonitschka Vagnerova on his conscience should be. And also those who let it happen, who pretended not to know what was going on. And then he had a vision of God. In return for the six years they were here, they should be made to work like devils for a million years in those Venezuelan mineshafts, with nothing on but their underwear.

3

"It's late," the cashier said to her mother. "The last performance is almost over."

"We'll have to sleep here in the dormitory," said the cashier later. "Downstairs there's someone from the railway we know. I don't want to risk walking home in the dark."

"I'm glad to hear you say it, my dear. But do you think they'll let us stay?"

"I can't say for sure, but I think they will," replied the cashier.

"What's making all that noise? It sounds like a generator somewhere underground."

At night it seemed to her that her mother was looking for the toilet, but she didn't know if it had been a dream or if her mother had really gone. She was already quite certain that the "unknown day" her mother was always talking about had already begun. In her mind—before she went to sleep—she saw the sweetshop. What was left of it looked like a woodshed. And there was the sign: "Death to German Swine." Outside she could hear intermittent bursts of gunfire and crowds of people moving through the streets. Why haven't I married yet? she wondered as she was falling asleep. Then she had three of her dreams, the kind she'd never tell anyone about: her indecent dreams, her indecent visions. She'd never have thought herself capable of such dreams. The blood rushed to her head whenever she thought of them.

In the first dream, the tall fellow's brother pressed close to her. It was before he'd exchanged her for Sonitschka Vagnerova, who was no longer alive. And he said to her, "I know what you want, what I want myself, what everyone wants. Sometimes there's so much else going on that love gets lost."

And then the tall fellow's brother said, "I feel we're together even though we aren't together and perhaps, since the Germans have killed so many of your people in the camps, we may not be. Your name alone is enough to warm, when I think about it or say it aloud. Sonitschka Vagnerova. Can you hear me, Sonitschka Vagnerova?" Suddenly, that scarcely familiar girl—known only by sight—had a voice, but she no longer had a face. What was her face like? She was pretty, that much is certain. Nicely dressed—that too.

And then Sonitschka Vagnerova answered the lanky fellow's brother and told him they ought not to have smashed up the sweetshop; and that she'd never, not even in the camps, have said that all Germans were swine, as though justice would have been served simply by turning over that sign banning Jews and scrawling a few different obscenities on the other side.

109

She felt as if she'd been touched by an invisible curse because of something her mother had done before she was born.

Her second dream was of a woman, ugly and fat. One night three men came to her door. The first said: "I have enough money to pay you to do everything." The woman replied that he would first have to do something for her. The man thought he hadn't offered her enough and stuck a roll of bills between her breasts. The woman laughed and pulled her blouse over her head, licked her lips and asked for more money. Then she told him what she wanted. The man refused. She said she couldn't force him, but if he were to leave he'd never know what he had missed. Then he left.

The second man asked how it had been. "Wonderful," the first replied. And the same thing happened to the next young man, whom she also rejected into the night. The third entered, an elderly man who was happy to have her tell stories. Only the cashier knew all the details, the words that were uttered, and the things that went on, the wrinkled face of the old man who'd come to her to get what he could not get. It was always the old men who wanted her to tell them how to live and how to die. Who can blame them for not wanting to die when they'd seen life before the war? How can they know when they're willing to pay nothing, neither with money nor with part of themselves? How do they expect to find out water is wet if they don't touch it? But she was laughing only with her mouth, not with her eyes, which looked like those of a piglet, clean from a fresh rain. "Everyone thinks the world was made for him; he doesn't remember that the world has been demanding the same favors all along."

Her eyes were grave, as if ten thousand years of wisdom and wrath and shame looked out from them. "What do they know about passion, which can destroy a person, silently and secretly?"

And then there was her third dream, about a red hole. The street was narrow, carved out long ago. Couples strolled the sidewalks, reading signs of invitation and stopping occasionally. Nothing to buy, they were told, but lots to see: girls, men, acts you'll never forget.

She woke and couldn't help thinking of her mother when she was young, and of what it was like to be up there, and what it was like the next morning when the raw, unswerving daylight flashed through the window and illuminated the recesses of the face.

Dreams were the cashier's freedom, as endless as a desert, a sea, a

night sky full of stars. Just as she was a living dream for her mother—
a dream of things that might be achieved or ways that fate might be
shaped—so were her dreams her own secret passions. They sparked and
fed on one another as if they were coal or wood, or a fire in the
wilderness, igniting bush after bush, tree after tree.

At the end of this, an image swept over the girl, as when the shooting
had begun outside. Tongues of blue and red licked her eyes, and then
she felt red explosions inside her. Suddenly the red became yellow. She
felt as if something were lifting her up and pushing her toward the
ceiling, as though it were her own hands, though she could no longer
feel them. She screamed silently. When at last all the colors had
vanished, black remained. But it was a soft black, like velvet, like a
caress. And when she woke up, she felt older than when she'd gone
to sleep.

She felt alone, even with her dreams. Her mother wasn't there. She
was afraid of the way her mother would look at her body. It didn't make
her feel good. And she thought about the massage salon that they'd
closed down. Who knows whether it was only because the manager
didn't pay his rent during the war? What went on there? Could she
imagine it?

In one of her fantasies she found herself in a room on the top floor
of the building with a view of the city at night. The room contained a
bed and a cot. The man, whom she'd met at the box office when he'd
bought tickets, lay on his back and she was sitting on a bench and a girl
knelt behind her brushing her hair. Nothing happened. There was a
quiet little song on the radio sung by girls' voices, about Sunday
morning. In the mirror on the ceiling she saw the reflection of flickering
candles and three people who didn't know each other and yet were
intimate friends.

She knew there had been a room like that in the former massage
parlor; once the cinema owner showed it to her. Could he possibly have
envied her because she was young, as her mother claimed? And once
she'd actually heard a song like the one in which girls sang of Sunday
morning, and it had made her feel like crying.

Outside, she could hear gunfire. It sounded like pistols or rifles.
Somewhere she heard a machine gun. Something seemed to go on down
below in the cinema, too. Perhaps the cleaning ladies had come early.
The railway men came and went. The trains arrived and departed

111

according to schedule, as though nothing unusual were happening. But the superintendent had closed the dormitory. There was also some excitement in the passageway.

She thought about the lanky fellow's brother and about Sonitschka Vagnerova. She connected it with what she sometimes thought about, how men and women are different between the legs. It seemed strange to her. Her mother was afraid, but she had her reasons. Everyone is afraid. The world is going through its final hour and I'm thinking about this.

Then, too, what disgusted her gave her pleasure at the same time. More than anything else, she wanted to touch—but only painlessly and without danger—an alien, incomprehensible world as intimately as she was touched by her own bedclothes. She felt the doors of paradise had opened for her, and she found that those same doors were also the doors of hell. From each tree you shall eat, save one tree, as she had learned in religion classes. She'd surrender to sleep with her new knowledge in the hopes that indecent dreams would come to her, regardless of whose life they belonged to. And then there was what the tall fellow had revealed to his brother: He'd wanted to lose his sex, the source of all his suffering.

The tall fellow used to go to Little Karlova Street to look at a mural painting of a monk who resolved a similar problem by cutting off the offending organ between his legs and throwing it to the dogs.

She could imagine her own picture on the walls of the buildings she used to walk past, though she had nothing to throw to the dogs but her fears, her terrors, her shame. The cashier dealt with her unanswered questions the way nearsighted people deal with their bad eyes. When she fell asleep—a deep sleep without the dreams, an empty sleep that gave her nothing and yet shamed her heart—it was to the accompaniment of music: either a waltz from the first act of *La Traviata,* so sad and beautiful that she felt like crying, or the aria from *Rigoletto.*

Where is Mother? What time is it? Maybe she's gone to the bathroom. She's left her shoes here. She can't have gone into the street in her stockings.

I'd like to love. I'd like to have my first love, even if it were the first and last love. Love—any love—at first sight or a quiet one, or maybe a stormy love so that men would make an effort for me. He'd understand my most secret signals and want to seduce me, court me, protect me, fight for me. I want to belong to someone, to stand at someone's side and have him at my side. To love a man more than my own life.

4

Walking along the corridor, the cashier's mother reached the emergency exit from the cinema, where she'd seen a light. Through the door, she could see two employees standing on the podium, on the audience side of the curtain. On the other side of the curtain, where the movie screen hung, stood a group of people, some in uniforms and some in civilian dress. An elderly man was talking to them. In the audience sat rows of German soldiers, deserters, with their hands tied behind their backs. The old woman gazed at the scene uncomprehendingly. Both orderlies were close enough for her to hear what they were saying, although they couldn't see her. She decided to stay and watch. Two other soldiers were guarding the prisoners. Except for the fact that one group was tied and the other held machine guns, there was no difference between them.

"You can rest the bench here for a while," said the first employee in a strong Sudeten accent. He was filthy from head to foot.

Only the safety lights were on. A draft came from an invisible window somewhere in a ventilation shaft. The first employee added: "Oh, God, what are they going to come up with now? Here, hold this for me."

He had a deep, hoarse voice. He paid no attention to the deserters whatsoever, nor to those guarding them, as though they didn't interest him in the least.

"*Dreckscheisse*," said the second man. "We're all *Tiermenschen*. Just take a look around you. We'd better hurry up and get out of here. The sooner we get this over with, the better."

"You don't say."

"No point in shooting your mouth off too much. They're fools. You can't mess around with them. They're using a wedge to drive out a wedge and nothing can stop them. We're all *Menschentiere*, like I say. And it won't be any different as long as things are in their hands. You know what's going on at home? Bakeries in Berlin are looted. Dispersed soldiers are organizing into Wehrwolf suicide units all over the Reich's territory. Americans captured the German gold reserves in the salt mines in Thuringia.''

"Reminds me of how we used to dig those ditches for silage back at the beginning," said the first. "Did you read *Schwartze Korps?* There's no sense in holding out militarily, but the idea must go on living under any hell."

He let the bench stand where it was, knowing that as long as he didn't lift his end, his colleague couldn't carry it alone.

"Except that they weren't meant for silage ditches. First they were fortifications, then they were graves. And we've got a million fresh men in this sector. Where will it end? But that doesn't mean I'm not going to be careful. What do you think they'll do with those fellows by the cloakroom?''

"How should I know?" said the first, but they both knew the answer. What they didn't know was how.

"If they can get three officers of the *Wehrmacht* or SS together, they have the right to condemn them for anything they want, and there's only one thing they want. They have the old man. He was sleeping upstairs. He's the judge." He began to whistle *Der Elefant von Indien.*

"Why don't they do it upstairs?"

"They know no one's going to come wandering into the theater in the middle of the night." Quietly he whistled *Kann das loch nicht findien* this time.

The mother looked at the bound German soldiers at the side of the auditorium, by the cloakroom; then she looked at the oak bench. There were so many deserters. She felt a buzzing in her ears; it was the underground generator again.

"Grab your end," said the second employee.

"Right."

"Take it easy, the staircase is narrow and I don't want to cripple myself after getting this far. I'm still planning to get home."

"Right, I'll treat her like a Chinese empress," said the first. "Or was it Japanese?''

It was a heavy oak bench that could accommodate twelve people at once.

The mother looked at the old man on the stage. He was gripping a golden tassel that was part of the dusty blue curtain. She felt as though midnight were sitting in her soul. As though the eclipse of the sun they'd written about in the papers were here already. She watched the employees handling the heavy oak bench with ease, like a toy. They were like draft horses. The one had stopped whistling.

The old man in a green hunter's outfit, the judge—probably with a private flat upstairs—watched the orderlies carry the bench onto the stage. They had already set up a table and two chairs with armrests. The old man was wearing plus fours and white woolen socks. He didn't look like a judge, though that was his profession; obviously he'd been just about to leave. Perhaps he really was going hunting.

Menschentiere, repeated the mother. That's a German word. *Menschentiere. Tiermensch. Tiermenschen.* What did they want to do with the soldiers? Why were their hands tied behind their backs? She shuddered. She could imagine only too well. They will kill them, because deserters aren't interested in *Lebensraum* anymore; they just want to go home. They don't want to shoot at people who never did anything to them, or even at those whose fault it all was. The two men she'd heard talking were Nazis at heart, and not just because of their uniforms and their insignia. The mother was overwhelmed by a sense of terror.

The old man looked delicate, and though erect, he gave the impression of barely being able to keep his balance. The expression of the first employee seemed to say: God, why are they dragging us into this? No one in his right mind would want anything to do with it at this point. The old bugger probably can't even wipe himself and flush the toilet without somebody holding his hand. And he's supposed to be watching over us?

"Lower it a bit, and I'll lift it up here," said the second employee.

The old man was looking for something in an open briefcase. It was a large, thick briefcase, the kind that the railway men used to carry their clothes and food. He pulled out a file with plans in it. The plans showed cellars and corridors, store rooms on the third floor where they kept the furniture and windows opening onto the street corners. The employees knew exactly where to put the bench. Now the open black briefcase stood beside the old man in the hunting outfit. The second employee, too, could scarcely bring himself to look at the old man, thinking: Can't he see that the water is rising, and those high-lace boots of his can't save him? He looks like he's ready for a trip to the mountains. Doesn't he know that the gravedigger is getting a grave ready for him not far from here, that the bell has already tolled?

115

The second employee, rather stout and not as grubby as the first, smiled respectfully at the old man.

The old man shifted the plans to his left hand, as though he were getting ready to point something out with his right. But it had nothing to do with them. He beckoned with his finger to a court secretary, who appeared to have just stepped out of bed. She was tired and unkempt, with a puffy face. It was already well past midnight.

"Yes, sir," said the first employee in his hoarse voice.

"I'm going to change," said the old man.

The mother had to strain her ears to hear. The old man looked at his large watch, which was on a gold chain that hung from buttonholes in his vest. He wound it up and then stuck it back in his pocket with trembling hands.

"Can you arrange it, please, miss?" he said to the secretary. "These two strong young men will be happy to help you with anything." The general should have been here already, he thought. But he didn't want to betray his nervousness. He went to a chair in the corner for his black robe. As soon as he touched the material, his listlessness seemed to disappear.

The stout employee sat down on the edge of the stage and let his legs swing back and forth over the floor with its footworn red runners. He pretended not to see the rows of seats full of soldiers. Whenever they brought in furniture for the stage, they came in from the left to avoid the cloakroom.

"Maybe he won't make such a big thing of it," said the first employee quietly.

"Life is not what you want but what you must do," answered the second. "Not what you expect, but what you've been ordered to do."

"Yeah, but now?"

"Didn't you hear shooting outside?"

"It's something else I hear."

The old man was explaining something to the secretary, who was listening with a sour expression on her face. He was telling her, in his soft voice, about the toughness that is the foundation of everything. We can do anything, miss, he reminded her, as though he thought she might have doubted it. "We are in the right, and we have our own will. We must demand toughness, miss, toughness and again toughness."

"Forget it," said the first employee a while later as he walked past the old woman, whose presence they either didn't suspect or didn't care about. "We should have gone over the hill long ago."

"Haven't you heard Germans don't die in bed?" said the second with a grin.

"It might well happen tonight, if not tomorrow."

"Be careful someone doesn't take you at your word."

"I could do with a cold potato right now."

"Let's clear out before they think up something else for us to do," said the second.

"Do you know what I saw in the cloakroom?" asked the first.

"Whatever it is, I'm not interested."

"Two of those doctors' handbags."

"So what?"

"So what do they need a doctor for?"

"How should I know?"

"I don't like it," said the first.

The mother watched as they walked toward the stairs where they'd brought the furniture down. They spoke in German so she could understand only vaguely. They pretended not to notice the soldiers. The soldiers were quiet. They couldn't have done much with their hands tied anyway, thought the mother. Oh, God, God, it's in the air, and what's in the air is killing. I don't have to be told that. We shouldn't have stayed here, and I'm afraid for my little girl, so I don't want to stay here and I don't want to go away, either. Why am I always so afraid? And if it's not death I'm afraid of, then it's life. Her skin settled in wrinkles she didn't have the day before. She looked at the stage from her hiding place. In his green hunter's outfit, the old man reminded her of "Little Red Riding Hood." I have midnight on my mind and in my soul, and I feel hot, as though this were somewhere in the Sahara. So my day has finally begun. She thought of when the Germans had first come and the newspapers had said that the time was past when anyone could attack defenseless German citizens and expect to get away with it. She'd also read somewhere that they were cultivating mushrooms for the Germans in the cellars of the Maginot Line. Those famous photographs in their magazines like *Der Stuermer* and *Der Angrijj* or *Der Adler*. The Germans had written that only those who'd suffered a just defeat could now have the audacity to demand peace. But they'd written that a long time ago. There must really be a generator whining away somewhere under the ground here.

The secretary was listening impatiently to what the old man was saying. Her nose was prominent and looked almost Jewish. She was bony but puffy. She probably found it hard to gain weight on a diet of lentils and black coffee, thought the mother. She's not as pretty as my little girl, whom I've looked after all through the war.

The old man snapped his fingers and wagged his trembling chin at the secretary. She glanced briefly at the soldiers with their hands tied behind their backs. They wore German uniforms and insignia representing various military branches. Most of them looked pretty slovenly. What the old man said hadn't sounded as grand as he'd intended. But the mother hadn't been able to hear what he said, except when he raised his voice.

"Who will keep the records, you?" the old man asked the secretary finally. "Where are those two musclemen who are supposed to bring you a typewriter? Have they gone? They probably think we need more chairs."

He turned to some people who were standing behind the curtain. She guessed from their voices that one was a woman, the other an officer.

The old man spoke to them: "What the Fuehrer had said . . . Anyone who would propose or even approve measures detrimental to our power of resistance is a traitor. He is to be shot or hanged without delay. I have here also my *Der Panzerbar* from the previous Monday. God is with us and our defense of the Reich. *Noch etwas, meine Herren. Jetz mussen wir uns ausheljen und vorlaujig die Tage des Ruhmes vergessen. Solange jedes unser Haus, jede unsere Wohnung und jedes Fenster eine Festung sist, so werden wir hier stark sein.*" The mother didn't get it, except for a few words.

The woman wore cotton stockings. She didn't betray what she was feeling by the slightest movement of her face. She might have been thirty. She told the old man she was a lawyer. She added something else and then said, "Mr. Chairman, I am here voluntarily." At the main station, she said, she'd seen the bodies of German families that had been shot and fortunately, she added, the bodies of dead bandits as well. About two hundred people on both sides had been killed. *"Ich wollte sie darum bitten, das ist das Gebot diesser Stunde."*

Several people in civilian clothes arrived with a man in the uniform of a colonel of the SS. That must have been the owner of the medical

base because the judge addressed him as "Herr Doktor." He shook
hands with the civilians and greeted the other officer in military fashion.
Both the civilians had hats with hunter's ribbons on them; the officers
had briefcases. The doctor requested that his two bags be brought from
the cloakroom. The civilians put on buttons bearing the insignia of the
National Socialist German Workers Party. It hadn't been a good idea to
wear them in the street.

The secretary summoned both employees and asked them to bring the
typewriter along with the doctor's bags from the cloakroom. Then she
sent them for one more table. The judge looked contentedly at those
present. His white collar was just a bit too tight for him. He had a
shriveled neck, like an old rooster.

"Close the door," said one of the men in civilian clothes to one of the
employees, pointing to where the mother was standing.

It turned out that among the civilians was a general out of uniform, which must have seemed strange to both officers present. The
judge bowed and said, "Herr General," as though he were dub-
bing him with the title. There was nervousness mixed with respect in
his voice.

"We have placed units of the defense police on watch at strategic
places, Mr. Chairman."

"*Jedem das seine,*" said the old man. To each his own. "I have
learned that the station and the approaches to the city have cost us the
blood of several dozens of our soldiers."

He took a tin box of digestive tablets from his side pocket and offered
them to the group on the stage, then closed the box again and stuck them
into his pocket.

"We are safe here," said one of the civilians.

"They are not unimportant provinces," said the general later.

The eyes of the old judge betrayed an effort to convince the others
that his loyalty, enthusiasm, will, and energy hadn't faltered. The cause
he'd devoted his life to would continue.

"These are mere rebellions that have not yet been suppressed. The
Empire is safe," said the old man.

His voice trembled. His whole body trembled. The palms of his hands
emerged from stiff white cuffs with mother-of-pearl buttons. The skin
of his hands was red, with brown and bluish blemishes. Blue veins
stood out on his skin in high relief, looking in places like ancient purple
strips. "Our laws are still in force here."

The cashier's mother became more and more convinced that somewhere deep beneath the floor a generator was operating. Her head ached. She could hear it even when the door was closed, although the noise was weaker then.

"Most of them are citizens of the Reich, not Hungarians, Romanians, or Ukrainians," said the first officer. He didn't look at the soldiers with their hands tied as he spoke.

"I'm only concerned about our families," said the old man. "Our apartments, however, are under military protection. I'm glad to hear our police are in the streets holding down strategic positions. That's just as it should be. So far, no evacuation order has been issued. Naturally we'll all remain at our posts—until the very last minute, gentlemen and ladies. In any case . . ." It was obvious that he had no doubts about his ability to convince the accused of their own guilt.

"Certainly," said the first man, who wore a green hat.

One of the soldiers with his hands tied was overcome with a fit of coughing. Several of them looked at him. He was almost choking. Something had become lodged in his throat and he couldn't get it out.

"We are the powerful," said the old man. And the rest in German, happily. "*So, Ich bin wirklich sehr glücklich, das Ich mit Euch bis zu Ende arbeiten und auch nuetzlich sein Kann. Alle sind wir hier.* I will take you all under oath, ladies and gentlemen. We shall proceed as the moment dictates. Gentlemen, arrange yourselves according to rank." The chain of his pocket watch swung back and forth on his stomach. "The purpose of the court is to issue verdicts. Of course."

Finally the soldier's coughing fit stopped.

From somewhere near the cloakroom, they led in more soldiers. A draft pushed the door open and the old woman could see some more of what was going on. The soldiers had obviously been beaten. She saw the two who had purchased the last tickets to that evening's show.

"You'll carry those who fall asleep to one side," said the doctor to both employees. He told them precisely where. When he was saying something that concerned the soldiers, he spoke succinctly, but more quietly.

"Should we wait here?" asked the first employee hoarsely.

The second employee looked as though he felt like vomiting. He turned pale, then red.

The colonel looked around and said to the second officer, "When it's over we can simply burn the place down. Have some gasoline brought in." He coughed without looking at the soldiers.

The judge looked as though the words had some kind of magic power. He could just imagine it. Nothing burned quite so well as gasoline. Gasoline burns even when it's damp. It burns in the rain and in the snow. The orderlies brought the gasoline up from the basement.

The doctor opened both his bags. They were full of hypodermic needles and bottles with all kinds of serum. The second bag was lined with vials of phenol. He counted the number of soldiers, including the new arrivals. He had serum enough for ten times as many. *"Menschentiere,"* the mother thought. They spoke in a fast German and she didn't catch everything and some things she didn't understand at all.

"Are you ready, miss? Is there paper in your machine?" asked the judge.

The man wearing an NSDAP pin turned to the judge. "Would you administer an oath to the employees?"

The old man in the hunter's jacket took a flag with a swastika and the sign of the sun on a reddish brown and white background from the second civilian and spread it on the table like a tablecloth. They had the first soldier brought up. It was the one who'd bought two tickets from her daughter, for himself and his friend. So they're starting with them, thought the old lady. What is that noise coming from the deepest underground? Generators? It sounded stronger and stronger.

It lasted a minute. Had he deserted in an hour of danger? Had he lost his unit, his platoon, his regiment, his division? Had he lost the whole German army? The old man pronounced him guilty. The doctor gave him an injection. He nodded to the employees. The secretary, the officers, and the civilians maintained intent, calm, matter-of-fact expressions. The general out of uniform seemed indifferent. The cashier's mother was holding her palms over her ears in order not to hear what sounded like generators in the center of the earth beneath her.

5

The cashier thought about her mother, about her indecent dreams, and about the shooting outside. She wondered where the lanky fellow's brother was and what they were doing with their stolen pistol. She could only hear occasional random sounds coming from the cinema. The cleaning ladies were probably finishing up. They always worked quickly, sweeping up the papers and cigarette butts and, sometimes, from the box seats, condoms. Sonitschka Vagnerova, the daughter of a used car dealer. She shuddered.

So Mother's day is finally here, she thought. But I'd like to know where those two brothers are. Maybe they're sleeping. Maybe they decided to go to bed and wait for morning. And morning can't be far away. The cashier could hear bird songs coming from the nearby river. The whole mess is collapsing and the world is still on its axis, the river is flowing and the birds are singing. Somewhere a dog barked. I wonder where the brothers are.

At that moment, they were on the other side of the river, and the lanky fellow's brother asked, "Do you see that stable?"

"Yeah," replied the lanky fellow. "But I also see they've got a soldier watching it."

"He looks tired. He's asleep on his feet," said the brother. He had his hand on the butt of the pistol. It was drizzling slightly and he didn't want the weapon to get wet, as though he believed the dampness would penetrate to the powder in the cartridges. Only eight rounds were in the weapon. The man who lost the pistol had already fired four of the twelve, and hadn't had time to reload the magazine.

"It's a wonder I'm not asleep on my feet, too," said the lanky fellow's brother. "I haven't slept for several nights. I've been talking with Sonitschka Vagnerova day and night. And when she started to tell me all that had happened to her, God appeared."

"Tell me about it later," the lanky fellow cut him off. "Let's not drag women into it. Let's not even drag God into it. Just concentrate on what we have to do right here and now. I don't even want to hear about how you don't need sleep. You can tell me all about it later."

"I'll tell you something about horses."

"Not now."

"And about dogs."

"Neither about horses nor about dogs, now."

They advanced along the railway track. At every bridge and crossing there was a soldier. The lanky fellow's brother thought: My God, they all look like scarecrows. These fools are guarding everything, even themselves, because they're scared shitless. Before, when they still had faith in themselves, five or six thousand Gestapo were enough to make nine million people tremble, the whole nation. As soon as they stopped believing, they started guarding everything, as though they thought people would steal their bridges and their railways in their own country. The fools. Do they keep an eye on each other when they take a leak? He remembered how they'd taken up railway tracks and shipped them to Germany.

"What are you looking for in the stable?" asked the lanky fellow.

"You don't know how much I like horses? And why?"

"Stop clowning around."

His brother looked up at the cloudy sky. All I have to do is think of you, Sonitschka Vagnerova, and I feel such a tenderness in my soul, like when I tense my muscles to lift a rock, the muscles in my arms, in my legs, in my chest or my shoulders. I have no words for it. Words make everything common. I'm charged with it, like these eight cartridges in my German revolver. As long as I think of you, I don't need sleep. God is with me. Isn't that right, God? As long as you were alive, everything was light inside me. Now that light has gone out. I search for the old fire but the only fire I have now is in my eight cartridges. That ticket girl looks a little like you, Sonitschka Vagnerova. I mean, she looks different, but who cares if she's light-haired and you had dark hair? When the Germans sang of blue-eyed maidens, did you seem different, special, set apart, because you have—had— walnut-colored eyes? Ever since yesterday evening when I met that girl in the passage, when I think of you, I also think of her. You'll forgive me, I know, because love is forgiving. Only hatred never forgives. Bitterness never forgives. Humiliation never forgives, as long as love doesn't take its place.

"The girl in the box office thought I was off my rocker when I told her I'd seen God."

"Maybe she wasn't far from the truth."

"Do you think I'm nuts for talking about it so openly like this?"

"I'd bet my life on it," whispered the lanky fellow. "Why don't you want to give me the pistol?"

"I've got a steadier hand than you do, I'm not as tall, and my knees don't have a habit of giving out on me. You'll get a rifle. Just give me time."

"I'll bet you're off your rocker," the lanky fellow insisted. His rabbitskin vest was as wet as his brother's. "What are you going to do?"

"You still don't know?"

"We don't need horses, that's for sure."

His brother looked at him with his cloudy eyes. I may not have had any sleep, he thought, but something else is giving me a headache. I'm soaking wet. He ground his teeth. He had strong teeth. If teeth were enough to chew your enemy to bits, he'd have no trouble.

The lanky fellow was holding a stick with a large hook attached at the end of it that looked like the arm of an anchor. His brother handed him the pistol, said he was going out there with his bare hands, and asked him to cover him. The soldier would see that he was unarmed and would be off his guard. Then the lanky fellow would step out of the dark with the pistol, and that would be that.

"This will be the first thing I've done for Sonitschka Vagnerova. So far I've only talked about it. Now comes the time for action."

"I'm surprised you're still interested," whispered the lanky fellow.

"We both know what we're doing," replied his brother. "It's raining. Not like in those mines in Venezuela. And if God is with me, I've got nothing to worry about."

He was interrupted by a train coming down the tracks. In the dark, it was a long time before they could tell what kind of train it was. It was moving slowly, a freight train with several wagons marked with red crosses. This was probably the main line, since the rails hadn't been torn up and sent to Germany.

"A hospital train," sighed the lanky fellow's brother. "Where's it going, Germany?"

"What?" asked the lanky fellow, leaning close to his brother. He could feel his hot, fetid breath.

"You can never tell whether a German train is coming back from a victory or a defeat. This one's probably coming from one of their Alpine National Fortresses, bringing the wounded and the dead. It's not an armored train, like they threatened on the radio last night."

"I can't hear you," said the lanky fellow.

"I'm off, while the train's making a racket."

"Go ahead, I'll cover you."

The tall fellow gripped the pistol in his fist and in the other hand held the pole with the hook attached to it. Both men stood up. They were wet to the skin. The lanky fellow shuddered.

"Hang on there," said his brother.

"Nothing to worry about."

"In a little while you won't be cold and neither will I."

"On your way."

The tall fellow's brother walked past the sleepy guard, who was hunched over in a standing position in a primitive guard hut with a wooden roof. The rain was falling heavily now, and it splashed into the hut through knotholes in the roof. The brother waited until the rain came down harder. Then he walked through the mud and puddles into the stable. The guard didn't notice him. He was huddled against the wall of his hut, where the rain couldn't reach him, and streams of water poured through the holes in the roof, making a noise that covered the sounds of the lanky fellow's brother going by him.

The stable smelled of last year's damp hay, of rotting leather, harnesses, barley or oats, and acidic horse urine. Chill breathed out of a stone trough, and lying on an oak bench, out of the reach of the horses, were horse blankets full of holes. Every once in a while the horses jerked when the fleas or damp flies irritated them. Dampness permeated everything. In the troughs lay the remains of a haystack; a pitchfork, leaning against the wall, stuck out of the hay. Besides the horses, urine and hay, there was a mousy smell there, cobwebs woven many years ago, and the sweetish smell of cats. Everything was wet and cool.

The tall fellow's brother stroked the horses only lightly with his large, coarse palm in order to make sure that these were horses and not just an illusion. He went from one horse to another, but he didn't touch the last one, the black stallion. He left the stallion out as if, by not touching him, perhaps he could make the stud not exist. He wanted to separate himself from the stallion, in this way at least. Even in the dark, the stallion's blackness stood out, though everything was enveloped in the shade and twilight.

The stable was empty except for the horses. Some began to whinny, but the guard didn't notice anything until later when the tall fellow's brother appeared in the stable door leading two white horses by their halters.

There's a feeling you get when entering a barn in the early morning, the tall fellow's brother thought, like walking in on some secret gathering. War or no war. Uprising or no uprising. Somewhere in the space between the shafts of light he could hear the movement of the animals. Suddenly, there was a commotion, and the many tiny birds that made their home in the barn during the rainy nights rose up in agitation and fluttered past him to the nearest exit. But the lanky fellow's brother's thrill came from the greeting he received. Stillness came to life and from each box appeared expectant, eager faces. These horses know me, he thought, they know my walk and my voice, in spite of the fact that I'm here for the first and last time. They've been waiting since dawn, since night, since the beginning of the war. I ask you, he said silently to the two white horses and aside to no one in particular, who else waits so eagerly for my arrival? Each horse greeted him; some neighed out loud, some regarded him silently and intently, but in all of their eyes, except for the ebony stallion's, he saw an openness and trust. He used a heavy chain lead which he twisted through the halter and brought under the chin, over the nose. This is one of the most sensitive parts of the horse's face. He could control each step of these thousand-kilogram animals with a jerk of his hand. An older horse boxed next to a lovely mare had probably spent hours watching her.

From the more affectionate horses there was a special greeting, a quiet nuzzle as he passed by, a touch that was intimate, honest, and kind. Not looking for the morning's ration of grain, they reached for a familiar word and stroke meant for only them.

Their bodies excited him and he loved to run his hands over their smooth powerful sides. It always amazed him that such a large animal could have such tender skin, responsive to the touch like a woman. He dreamed of horses often and they always reminded him of women: strong women, moral and independent; soft women, conquerable with patience and gentle hands. But he liked to think that every spirited horse, like every woman that ever lived, could eventually be won over; though they could face brutality and roughness with fierce animal vengeance. Shaggy and coarse, they turned their large watchful eyes on him, an intruder in the early dawn.

He loved huge draft horses, he thought, but then he loved all horses. Their eyes gave them away. He'd approach each one and look for the gentleness in the soft folds of their eyelids. Beyond that, a light in the dark depths of the eye itself would reveal intelligence and trust. But the black stallion had the unreadable eyes of a hard woman whose suspicion and distrust radiate from inside. The body would be warm and supple to the touch, but the eyes remained dead. He saw the eyes of death.

The lanky fellow was watching the guard and saw his astonishment at what his brother was doing with the horses. He saw him raise his rifle, its bayonet fixed, ready for firing. Everything was covered, watered down by the rain. My brother is nuts, thought the lanky fellow. He has cloudy eyes and he's been nuts ever since they locked up that Jewish girl from the used car lot. Sonitschka Vagnerova. But he'd never even spoken to her. He'd only seen her from a distance. He doesn't even know her. And she definitely doesn't know him; she never had the chance to. My God—they were from different sides of an abyss, deeper than all the abysses of the world put together. And by now she is probably dead. Dead as a Jewess.

So he really has gone off his rocker. But he did manage to get the pistol, and that's what counts now. Whoever has a pistol has a chance to do something. He has only two things in his head—that Jewish girl and revenge. His obsessive notion of justice. They keep changing placcs in his mind, likc thosc submarincs with chambcrs that fill with water to submerge and then fill with air to surface, over and over and over. He's nuts.

The tall fellow saw his brother spit in the mud in front of the German soldier. Both of them looked like wet hens; only the horses looked beautiful in the rain. Even in the dark they looked magnificent. Horses are the most beautiful animals in the world. They're neither too large nor too small. They are beautiful, like everything that's just the right size. And at night they look as though they were made of darkness itself.

The brother walked to the corner of the yard and tied both white horses to a tree. A leaky wooden barrel stood by the tree, and the lanky fellow thought about the ways in which a man is like that barrel, of how for six years the German occupation had got on his nerves and why Friday was the last day—today was Saturday—and why it's like a barrel that can hold no more rain. The guard might have thought the lanky fellow's brother worked for the stable. The brother disappeared into the stable once more, but he left the doors open and immediately afterward led two bays out and tied them up to the tree by the overflowing barrel. Altogether he brought out eight horses in this way. The lanky fellow counted them. Back in the stable, he caught a glimpse of a black stallion which his brother hadn't untied. They were racing horses. They probably belonged to some German officers.

The soldier was watching the brother from his guard hut and had probably decided it was time to ask him why he didn't leave the horses in the stable. But the lanky fellow's brother knelt down in the straw at the edge of the stable and unrolled a waterproof piece of canvas that he'd tucked inside his vest. He thought of the underground mines in Venezuela, where it's so hot that people sweat blood and urine, until at last they sweat out their hearts and their souls, for Sonitschka Vagnerova.

"Sonitschka Vagnerova," said the lanky fellow's brother—and the soldier didn't know who he was talking to—"you were as beautiful as those curtains when I looked down from the hill onto your balcony and into the back room where you slept. And you were sweet as candy. Because of you I feel enough strength in each arm to lift a hundred kilos without my legs giving out. Only yesterday I could scarcely have lifted twenty without both hands."

The lips of the lanky fellow's brother moved without his saying anything. He spoke only for himself, like a ventriloquist. I love you, Sonitschka Vagnerova. Your love for me and my love for you is like a gorgeous fire that warms and shines on everything, but doesn't burn. Love is a fire, in which everything that makes a man and our lives dirty burns to ashes without dirt, choking smoke coming out of it. You cannot therefore ever die and disappear from the world as if you never existed.

"How would you like to lay off that," said the lanky fellow quietly to his brother, when he saw what he was up to, but there wasn't anything he could do to stop him. The soldier finally went to see what he was doing and to whom he was talking.

The bundle of straw caught fire and the brother stood up. The first wisp of smoke curled up into the air and out of the stable, where it mingled with the rain and sank to the ground.

The ebony stallion in the back of the stable roared like an animal does when it senses a fire or a flood or an earthquake. It was a terrible sound and the other horses by the tree outside took it up. The stallion began to kick out around him, jerking to pull himself loose. The lanky fellow's brother was struck by the power of the animal. Where's the heavy chain? You could tell how the horse had been handled because of welts and the swollen uneven profile showing on the face of the stallion. Where was the chain lead?

The hard eyes wouldn't soften and the dilated nostrils didn't relax. The boy both admired and feared the horse, and therefore hated him.

The soldier ran quickly into the stable and started to untie the stallion. He began shouting at the lanky fellow's brother, who stood up and, in the midst of the fire that was rapidly spreading through the stable, spit in the soldier's face. The soldier raised his rifle with the fixed bayonet, ready to lunge at the brother, but was paralyzed by the sight of this madman. The brother slapped the soldier's face hard on both sides. And as the soldier jerked forward, the lanky fellow stabbed him in the side with the hook. Like the tine of an anchor, the hook lodged in the soldier's body and couldn't be pulled out. With every movement he made, the hook did more and more damage to his body.

"Pick up his gun," said the lanky fellow. "I don't want to shoot unless I have to. We might bring someone running."

Both of them were lit by the fire. They were surrounded by the whinnying of the horses and the anguished cries of the black stallion, which had finally managed to pull itself free and rushed like a maddened creature out into the rain and night, where it ran around and around the yard until it finally tired and stopped, exhausted and perspiring, beside the other horses, which were glowing in the light of the fire.

They saw they were alone. Thanks to the rain, the fire didn't spread beyond the stable. When it died down, they could smell only smoke in the rain.

"We're alone here," said the lanky fellow's brother. "I'd be happier if she could have seen it."

"Who, that girl in the box office?"

"Sonitschka Vagnerova."

"How would you like to lay off that for a while."

"I'll let the horses go. Maybe our people can round them up. If I knew how to ride, I'd ride till the earth shook clear through to Venezuela. They could hear the thunder of their hooves down in those hot mines under the earth. Those eight light-colored horses are all right. The black one is a devil. I was afraid to touch him but I finally managed to tie him up tight. But you can't tie the devil down. You heard it yourself. He roared like the devil."

He thought of the soldier lying in his own blood, which was running out into the mud and the water. "He tried out his bayonet attack on me, just like their defense police. They teach them to do it that way. Nothing like this will come back anymore."

"Come on, we'll talk about it some other time."

"Do you want the pistol or the rifle? You can keep the hook," said the lanky fellow's brother, and then took his pistol back. They hadn't even fired it.

The rain had slowed to a drizzle once more. It was almost morning. On the way the lanky fellow's brother said, "Do you know how cold it must have been in Poland when it froze, and how hot when the sun shone? Just like those mines in Venezuela."

"Keep your discoveries to yourself," said the lanky fellow. "You'd end up reminding me of Goebbels and the murder of those Polish officers in Katyn. Forget it for a while. We've got too much else to worry about. This is a fantastic German gun. Is this what they called *scheisse?* We can go back to the dormitory. We'll get sorted out there, and see what to do next. The girl's there."

"Right," said his brother, and he thought: I hope she isn't jealous of Sonitschka Vagnerova, even though they're both beautiful. But that girl must still be a virgin because her mother won't let anyone lay a hand on her. She keeps her safely wrapped up in cotton wool. As though she felt her virginity weren't between her legs, but in her head, in those eyes that always look so frightened.

"You know what Sonitschka Vagnerova told me? That there are no happy endings in life, just happy stations. Life is an ugly joke. You must accept it, though, and bear it with dignity. It's the dignity that's the hard part. But happiness isn't always in stations, either. It's sprinkled throughout, and we live by looking from one sprinkle to the next. If it comes, it goes away fast, causing more panic than before."

"Yeah."

"They started with their own weak people."

"Yeah."

"Am I not a lucky stiff?"

"Till the death," said the lanky fellow's brother as they went on their way.

6

Soldier Number 9 stood before the doctor, the officer and the civilians in hunters' fedoras with ribbons and feathers in them, and the old man's black judicial robes lay tossed across the chair beside him. He looked at his flat pocket watch on the gold chain. It was almost five in the morning. This was the second soldier, the companion of the one who'd bought tickets for the last show the night before. After the first had been sentenced, they'd started at the other end. The judge wiped his lips. They wouldn't be finished as quickly as he'd reckoned, he thought, because they'd brought in more soldiers. But these were probably the last, because in the meantime the telephone wires had been cut. They had lost contact. The soldiers were lined up like sheep. Not only were they imprisoned here, but they had imprisoned themselves from inside.

The cashier's mother stood frozen to the spot. She'd forgotten about time. She narrowly avoided being seen by the employees as they brought cannisters of gasoline from the garage. She was listening to the underground generators.

"Who are you?" asked the judge in a tired voice. "Where have you left your weapon?"

The employees dragged aside a soldier who'd been put to sleep with an injection. They did it the same way they'd dragged the furniture into the cinema earlier in the evening.

The old man pulled out the box of lozenges and offered one to the general: "Would you care for a mint?" he asked politely. "They don't even know how morally crippled they are."

Then he turned to the soldier and went on, "Do you have your identification with you? And do up your buttons and straighten up your clothes. A uniform is a symbol. Don't you know how to behave properly before a military court?" With some difficulty, he unfastened his pocket watch from his vest and lay it on the table in front of him. "Do you still have papers, or have you sold them or thrown them away?" He tried to raise his voice and shout, but it sounded like the shrieking of a child.

His chin sank to his chest. Now it seemed he had no chin at all. He began to wind his watch; then something happened. Maybe he'd broken a spring. A good thing I'm sitting down, he thought. He had a very small head, like a child's. "Didn't they warn you what would happen if you lost or sold your weapon?" So his old pocket watch had finally given out. How long had he had it? Fifty-two years.

The rest of the people in the court, through their expressions and whispering, showed their displeasure at the old man in the hunter's jacket and plus fours for having lost a sense of time and proportion, and even for having lost his inventiveness, because he was still waiting for the soldier's reply. Finally the soldier said, "They robbed me and beat me. Then I ran into a buddy and we went to the movies."

131

"Do you know what you can expect?" asked the judge.

"I couldn't help it. They beat me. I was outnumbered. They stole my weapon."

"No need to deliberate over this one, gentlemen," said the judge. The folds of skin on his throat trembled.

The secretary watched the judge's mouth, as though she were taking dictation. Her face was even more swollen than it had been at the beginning. Her sheeplike back was bending.

Power has only a beginning and an end, thought the general. It has no middle. Power cannot bear moderation. The doctor thought only about how many vials of serum he had left in his bag. The judge thought about his pocket watch. Those two employees should be given something strong to drink so they won't wear themselves out. Both civilians looked at each other and, after a silent agreement, removed their NSDAP pins.

"We'll give you a shot for energy," said the second officer to the soldier, who looked about suspiciously, as if he wanted to attack someone despite his hands being tied. They untied him and he didn't move.

"Sign this for me here," said the doctor.

It took him a while. They let him take his time.

It was, as the mother saw, only a matter of technique. They put him in a chair, told him to roll up his left sleeve and hold out his arm, and cover his eyes with his right hand. He'd be given a pick-me-up shot. Fruit sugar. And then an antityphoid shot. They'd inject that straight into his heart. What can it be? the mother asked herself. What do they shoot into their hearts that makes them die so suddenly? They look as though they were asleep. It reminded her of the way they kill old, sick, or wounded dogs that are beyond help.

The secretary had lit some candles when the telephone wires had been cut. Now, when the electric lights suddenly went out, it became evident how much foresight she'd had. Suddenly the noise from the underground faded. So it must have been a generator, thought the cashier's mother.

The guards struck matches, but they needn't have worried, for the prisoners had nowhere to go, though the noise of men suddenly shifting in their seats came from the audience.

"You will all be transferred to the Reich," said the judge. "Take them away."

The prisoners could hear nothing and they were surprised by the silence, the absence of shooting.

They sentenced all those on the stage who now were lying side by side, a row of corpses behind the curtain. The old woman could see only a portion of what was going on.

The judge half-closed his eyes, but it was the old woman who seemed to see only the candle flames and the deserters lying beside each other. The judge stared at the dead men and his chin began to tremble again. The old woman thought of dead dogs and wondered why the Germans had created words like *Menschentiere* and *Tiermenschen*.

"Pull yourself together," said the general to the soldier.

The expressions on the faces of the civilians showed they were lost in their own private thoughts. But something was happening. The old man's eyes appeared to bug out. He caught himself by the throat and chest, and then appeared to stiffen. His will was broken. It was as though he no longer wanted anything. All of his energy had evaporated. The box of lozenges fell from his hand and, for a moment, his watch could be heard rolling away into the silence. The old man had apparently had a heart attack. The trial was over. The doctor closed his bags. Those who had taken part in the trial went to the cloakroom and ordered the guards to leave with them. They also told the employees to leave everything as it was and go. The general and the second civilian stepped aside to allow the doctor, who was carrying a medical bag in each hand, to leave first. Suddenly the cinema was empty. The old lady looked at the candles, the old man and the dead soldiers. She was wearing a wrinkled black mourning dress and she stared into the dark.

She was thinking how quickly the world had changed in a few hours, and about the plague. About what she'd heard of the plague from her mother and father, at school and from the talk of people. She also thought about the rats and mice who spread the plague. The judge, his people on the stage, the deserters, and their guards in the audience made her think of the plague, even though they didn't have swollen glands or high fever.

That's what rats are after: if they themselves must die, then no one should live.

Suddenly, the soldier with the chafed neck stepped from behind the heavy black velvet curtain and grabbed the old man, the judge, who blinked as though he were waking up, then opened his eyes wide. He felt the soldier gripping him. Then something in his body crunched. Again, his head fell forward. He blinked like a terrified bird.

"My God," said the old lady.

The old woman's words fell into the silence of the cinema. The soldier with creases and raw red patches on his neck sat down on the bench. He looked at the flag draped over the long table and at the bench, now empty, and at the judge. He thought for a moment about what to do with him. The old woman was finally able to pull herself away from her spot at the emergency exit. She went back toward the dormitory to see if her daughter was still sleeping. She could hear the spluttering of the candles as they burned down and were extinguished in pools of wax.

7

At five o'clock in the morning, just when it was beginning to turn light, about five minutes before her mother returned, the cashier left the building. She intended to look for the lanky fellow and his brother. She wanted to go by herself, not because she was afraid for her mother, but because she wanted to do something on her own to show that her mother need no longer worry about who would look after her when she no longer could. But the cashier talked with her mother in her mind and told her, Yes, you were right, it's like an infectious disease. We all have it, as though something were being handed out for nothing and even people who don't need it want it, because normally you have to pay for it with your own skin, with your neck, but now it's free. A little piece of something everyone is fighting over. The Germans really did make *Tiermenschen* out of people.

She also felt she was rushing into something she only half understood and, at the same time, she feared. But, like a flash of light, it wasn't to be missed.

It was a pleasant spasm, not unlike when you touch yourself and long to be touched by someone else—an unknown someone—a man you may not even be fond of, since until that moment you hadn't known him.

She might have gone to see the owner of the cinema, but she knew he had locked himself in as soon as she'd turned in the money from last night's three shows and not even a pair of Belgian draft horses could drag him out now. The only men she knew, apart from those in her fantasies, were the lanky fellow and his brother. Why should anything happen to me? Even though it wouldn't necessarily be unpleasant, she thought. All night long she'd tried to determine what the sounds coming from the different quarters of the building were—from the cinema, the dormitory, the garage. She was cold; she needed something to keep her shoulders warm in the morning. An afghan, or at least a blanket. It's better to be outside than to have to put up with dreams about old men who couldn't understand her, who thought she was an easy woman like all women, and simpleminded, who thought that every woman or girl would do everything. But that, too, was far away, like the roses strange men, at this very moment, may be offering to strange women, as they contemplate an invitation to go on an outing, to a hotel, to a spa, or to Paris, which even during the war was like a vast amusement park, or so they said on the radio.

The cashier no longer thought about how she'd open herself up to everything a woman could if she were approached by someone she could only have dreamed about all those years with her prudish mother. Those blue pools or bluish spots that swim at the bottom of her eyes when she thinks about it, and her hands, not the hands of a man, do with her what comes of itself. And then the red explosions that burst to the surface and suddenly transform red to yellow and invisible hands grasp her and lift her to the ceiling, which she will touch with her hand and cease to feel. Inner cries join in and finally black, velvet black, like a soft and tender caress, like when you're touched by the soft tips of invisible fingers.

She was fortunate enough to have blue eyes and fair hair and she knew what a passport that was, allowing her to breathe, walk, exist. Survive.

She walked past the demolished sweetshop where not even a teaspoon or a light bulb remained because everything had either been looted or broken.

This was something she both deplored and approved. It disgusted her, yet she agreed with it. It made her feel a horror and an enthusiasm she didn't understand. The *Lebensborn* organization was given a palace on the other side of the Vltava to which they brought girls from France, Germany, Norway, and many Czech girls about whom very little was known. After Heydrich's assassination there were orphans wherever you looked.

So the tall fellow's brother is taking Sonitschka Vagnerova with him into the revolution, she thought. But no one is taking me; I must bring to everything the swirling confusion I feel within me.

She was passing by the House of Romania bar. Last winter she had gone there with her mother. The Gypsy had sung a song called *Fire*.

> Even in the darkness of my village
> A part is missing from my body
> Oh, it's withering away, and hurting
> My body's on fire
> Oh, I still want to love
> Even if I burn to ashes

She would never forget the song.

The cashier was dreaming about love she never learned of, love the gypsies sang about, love so strong that people would kill for it without feeling guilt. Only the image of such passionate love, for which one is able to die, betray, and desert everyone and everything, all people and all things, hypnotized her. It was as if she were in a trance. She had a feeling she was losing her balance. An expression of single-mindedness, of looking inward, came into her eyes. God, I hope I don't faint here, she said to herself. She didn't. She only appeared to be enchanted, as if she were walking through a world other than that of the Prague pavement, with her pale face, blue, unseeing eyes, and her angel-blond hair.

The entirety of her mother's advice, even the color of her mother's voice, whirled around in the mind of the cashier, who would prefer an unhappy love to no love at all. Why did her mother think so badly of men?

Oh, my little girl, she could hear her mother in her mind. The fabricated nonsense that men devise against women, and dumb women against themselves, doesn't last, even in the most magnificent of affairs. It's nothing but a trap—some money or a mountain of impossible wishes and unfulfilled promises. It's like walking barefooted across a frozen river, on thin ice, my little girl. Nobody shares anything when he doesn't have to. Don't let them make you believe anything about the human heart where it concerns men, or money, or the future. It's only your sweet body and their pleasure seeking, little girl. After they get what nature condemned them to, they feign not having the time, as if it would be a greater sin to lose another second with you. Business, war, the job of a streetcar driver or a conductor are like a thicket for them in which they want to hide. They'd rather go to war than stay with you for another minute. I don't want to blaspheme. What they call passion, you'll forget all about it long before you grow old. It has no echo, like bad perfume, or cheap garters. It is yesterday's sunset, last year's snow. Oh, if I weren't ashamed to tell you what I have been, what I have gone through, what I had to do for money in order to be helpful to you a little. We are spared nothing, my little girl. You have to be practical, and understand that love will not wrest you out of your loneliness. A family? The foreman on the construction project next to the Adria Palace told me: It's good to have a family and a house like a castle. But then build a back door and sneak out. Oh, child, even what looks at first glance like the happiest family is a nest of treason. Men will sleep with just about anything, even animals.

The cashier felt shame wrapped in fear, like a piece of headcheese enveloped in greasy paper. And worry, which in turn was cloaked in the courtesy, restraint, and decency required of young women. She couldn't get over her fear of being despised.

There was a woman who came to the cinema once a week and bought a ticket from the cashier. She was pretty and always well dressed, but the cashier knew she wasn't employed, so she could guess how she made her living. Later she found out the woman lived in a nice three-bedroom apartment in Carpenter Street, on the third floor, with an advisor to the Minister of Justice, an older man whose mother wouldn't allow him to marry this woman. She was always very friendly to the cashier. She came once a week to the cinema, always by herself, and she and the cashier spoke a little each time she came, so they became acquaintances. The woman fascinated her.

Sometimes the cashier would tell officers the box wasn't available (her mother would have fainted on the spot, had she known) or she would say to herself that if she were forced to choose between giving the box seat to Sonitschka Vagnerova or her new acquaintance, she would not have hesitated for a second.

She tried to imagine—even now, as she was walking—what it would be like to be that woman.

The cashier was glad it wasn't her life, yet she envied her. It was like a magnet that attracted and repelled her at the same time, a force that tugged at her body and mind, her veins and her bones.

But the outcome of all the cashier's thoughts was that the dead Sonitschka Vagnerova, without any personal guilt in the matter, had taken from her the man she was thinking about and whom she wanted to see, even with his murky eyes. It was a fortunate thing he'd told her where he and his brother would be, so she could find him.

For a while she thought about the small salamanders and frogs she'd collected as a little girl in the puddles left by autumn or spring rains. The tiny tree frogs had eyes like bits of glass. They were no bigger than a child's thumbnail. Their eyes were angular.

She thought about Sonitschka Vagnerova, who even in death was fortunate enough to have someone in Prague think about her, for whom she is like the sun. She at least was worthy of being transported, but what am I worthy of? But then—oh, no, thought the cashier. I can't envy the poor thing in her death. Or can I?

She thought about her mother. I always felt disgusted when you silenced me all the time, Mother. My little darling, my honey. The cashier shuddered. A cold wind was blowing up from the river. She sensed what she was afraid of and why she was comparing herself with the dead Sonitschka Vagnerova. And then she heard the sound of her mother's voice, and the voice said: I haven't sung for a long time, dear. And she sang a few chords from *Danube Waves* and then burst out crying. Why are you crying, Mother? Other people are happy. That's why, my precious girl. Because other people are happy. I want to be like others. I want to join in. In my mind I hear a song about being together, about how we keep together. There must be a door to enter, Mother, isn't it so?

How can you be happy when you're afraid of everything? How can you be happy when the nearest person is so far away? When people hurt each other, even when they don't want to, even when they're not aware of doing it? It's so easy to hurt someone else. Do you think I don't know that, my sweetheart? I feel guilty and I don't know why, said the cashier. And she laughed at herself and saw all those colors once more, including black, which was like velvet and meant caressing.

Everyone is hidden as if in a box which is impossible to open. One cannot live this way. I don't want to live like this. And, with every move of her white arms, with her every stride, with a clenching of her hand into a fist, she went straight ahead, as if she were opening the doors to somewhere, to another place, where she would live her own life.

She thought about why people did what they did: the things the movie theater owner did in order to grow rich, and the lanky fellow's brother, in order to be remembered should he be hit by a bullet, sought danger in order to reassure himself and the others that he was no worse than the Germans. Her mother wanted her to meet a man who would make up for what Mother never got.

A moment later, in the window of a five-story apartment building in Parizska Street, she saw someone, probably a German woman, waving a white flag. The woman was about thirty years old and she wore a green German army sweater. At first the cashier didn't know whether she was surrendering or signaling someone. She remembered the sweetshop. Those signs. "Death to German Swine." "No admittance to Jews." And then it occurred to her: I probably shouldn't cross. And she didn't, because just then shooting started. Suddenly she could neither advance nor retreat. This is a silly thing to be doing, she thought, but I knew I'd end up like this. Absently, she stroked her lovely fair hair, washed in the chamomile her mother gathered each summer. Like an echo in her mind came the thought that she hadn't succeeded at much of anything in her life, and this wasn't just because the Germans had been in the land for the last six years. And she thought: I'm still pretty, but perhaps not as pretty as I used to be; and I'm a virgin. And she thought of what that meant.

She stopped on the corner. No farther, instinct told her. Not another step.

Something made the cashier's ears buzz. The German woman was no longer in the window. From the lower end of Parizska Street, from the direction of the Vltava River, an armored vehicle on tank treads crawled toward the center of the city like a caterpillar. It was a Hackel, firing toward the town hall from its cannon. A girl who looked like a peasant grabbed the cashier around the shoulders and drew her sharply in towards her.

8

"Don't give them your body to shoot at," said the country girl. "We're not here for a fashion show, miss." And then she said, "Since you're here, hang onto this thing for me, would you?"

She pressed a bazooka into her hand. It was heavy, and the cashier had trouble holding it. "It weighs enough," she said.

With some people she tried to make her conversation sound like dialogue she might have heard in a film. But this time it was her own voice, and she felt as if she were hearing it for the first time in her life.

"It does that," replied the country girl. "It penetrates even the thickest armor plate and explodes only inside the tank."

She adjusted something on her skirt and then took the weapon back. She grabbed the bazooka's wooden handle as though she'd been in the army for years. The cashier's hands felt empty. Something had happened at last, she felt, even though it wasn't much. It was a beginning. Something that was flowing towards her like the Vltava River. It was different from how she felt when the owner of the cinema had said she should experience something before it was all over, but what he meant for her to experience was himself. No hard feelings, miss, whatever you'd like. Who knows what's coming, miss. He had a dog. It reminded her of the time her mother had taken her to visit a family that had three dogs. They stank terribly. The family pretended that the smell was all part of having dogs.

"Don't be afraid," said the country girl, or perhaps she was a city girl who merely looked as though she were from the country. She sounded as if she really believed there was nothing to be afraid of, and not just as if she were trying to convince herself.

"Of what?"

A burning wall of the clock tower on the town hall came crashing down in front of the former grave of the Unknown Soldier, which the Germans had removed. The armored vehicle continued to fire at regular intervals.

The country girl put the bazooka down on the sidewalk and tried to pull up a manhole cover. The cashier thought for a moment and then went to help her. In doing so, the girls put themselves directly in the vehicle's path, but it continued to fire at the town hall. Maybe they were trying to destroy their archives, the lists of traitors. The cashier grabbed her side of the manhole cover with lovely white hands and prayed to God to give her strength to help the other girl lift it, because it wouldn't budge. The stench from the sewer reminded her of the cinema owner's dog, of those three dogs of the family her mother had taken her to visit, and of the lanky fellow's brother's two dogs, one dead and one still alive. Finally they managed to loosen the cover, but they still couldn't move it to one side so they could climb down inside the sewer. There were no men around, or rather there were, but they were on the other side of the street and they couldn't cross as long as the armored vehicle kept firing.

The apartment building where the woman had stood in the window with the white flag had apparently been evacuated. It wasn't until a machine gun started shooting that the girls realized a firing post had been set up there.

Suddenly everything seemed laughable to the cashier, though not enough to make her want to laugh out loud. She could smell the stench of the sewer and the smell of the river in the distance, the fragrance of the fields and the hillsides with their trees and parks. But mainly the stench. By the Law Faculty Building, where a German garrison was headquartered, a platoon of riflemen in full field gear, helmeted and armed to the teeth, was moving into action.

They finally managed to free the manhole cover. The country girl was red with the effort. The veins in their necks stood out. The tank, still firing, was coming closer and closer. The gunner was still aiming at the tower and walls of the town hall, but he had only to dip the cannon and swing it to one side to pulverize them as though they'd never been born. If the vehicle continued on its way, it would drive through the town hall as through butter, and the flames wouldn't harm it.

When they finally slid the cover off the hole, the stench of the sewer seemed like the sweet smell of a park, and the iron, rough and dirty with more than rust, seemed smooth. They scarcely noticed the rough edges that scraped their skin until they bled. The bazooka made of wood and iron lay inert beside the manhole. The riflemen were advancing behind the tank towards the town hall from the Law Faculty Building, where others were now fighting.

The country girl climbed down the ladder into the manhole. She did so nimbly, though there was scarcely room to move. The cashier didn't hesitate. The girl in the country dress, with the body and face of a peasant, was already covered by the stone shaft, and the cashier moved as quickly as she could to get inside as well. She understood what was going on, even though most of her understanding was only approximate, but what did that matter? Something told her this was how it should be. She no longer thought of Sonitschka Vagnerova, or of how the dead can steal men away from the living; she didn't even think much

141

about her mother. She was utterly absorbed in what she was doing with her new acquaintance, whose name she didn't even know.

Until this moment, she thought, nothing has worked out for me, but now we'll see. She realized she was no longer conversing in her mind with her mother, only with herself.

"Hand me that thing," said the country girl. "Carefully."

When the cashier grasped the main part of the bazooka and handed it down so that her new friend could fire it, the country girl repeated her warning.

"Come down a bit lower, it'll be easier for you," said the country girl. "You can hang onto me. I won't fall now. Come here beside me. I'll try to fire it."

"My God," said the cashier, as though she doubted the country girl could actually work the contraption. She had to shout to make herself heard. The country girl didn't seem to notice her, but only in the way we don't notice people to whom everything unites us.

Gases were seeping from the sewer, reminding her again of when her mother had taken her to see those people with the smelly dogs. Below them flowed a river of sludge, with bubbles popping on the slimy surface. At night, when no one was looking after them, the dogs probably made messes all through the flat, thought the cashier.

"Come on," urged the country girl. "They're too close already."

The tank was coming nearer. The country girl had a pimply complexion and green eyes with circles under them that cut deep into her face. She held the butt of the weapon. She began to hiccup.

It occurred to the cashier that the peasant girl was holding the weapon like a kitchen utensil. Like what? Ah, she thought. And then there was a roar that filled the street where the men were standing.

The girl above her crouched down and fired. The whole thing, including the explosion, lasted about two seconds. The cashier expected everything to explode—windows, cobblestones, the wide avenue that suddenly looked like a field of blood. Then, in the third second, came the reverberation, spreading through the underground corridor of the sewer. A wave of pressure poured over them. The cashier thought she had opened her eyes, but they were closed the whole time and she saw nothing at all.

She thought she saw the country girl and her own mother and the lanky fellow before her. They were all lying together, but the lanky fellow's brother lay with Sonitschka Vagnerova. They exchanged a few words. Someone was covered with blood, a face was tightened in pain. Everything was dark and then brightened before the cashier's eyes. She didn't see the woman in the sweater in the fifth-floor window firing a military pistol, round after round, towards the sewer from where the country girl had successfully fired her first bazooka and blown up the tank. The woman kept firing, even though the tank was already in flames with its crew still inside it. The cashier felt as though she were hanging dead from the ladder, and she saw all the colors. No more than ten or twelve meters away, the tank was in flames and the metal was turning red hot. It was like when she'd come here, alone but to be less alone, and she thought of the colors that sprang from her memories, from recollections of something beautiful, of being happy, even though it had never happened. Only the colors remained. Only then did she remember her mother. Regret filled her. And that was all she remembered.

9

The cashier's mother sat on a chair until eight o'clock and waited. It had begun on Saturday, and then it was Sunday, and then Sunday evening and then Monday, but now she didn't know what day it was. It's not over yet, she thought. No one has to tell me, I can hear it from the street and I know what's going on from what happened in the night. She'd worn the same black widow's dress for several days, and she hadn't changed her underthings. She hadn't changed anything. She could wash and change her clothes when it was all over, when the other day came. Who knows what's become of my darling little girl, my precious little girl. I hope nothing bad has happened.

Shortly after nine the lanky fellow and his brother appeared in front of the box office, which was closed. Both wore red arm bands with the letters RG on them, for Revolutionary Guard. The lanky fellow had a fever and a rifle with a bayonet, and his brother had a pistol stuck in his belt. The pistol was visible whenever he opened his rabbitskin vest, by now beginning to fall apart, as the cashier's mother had predicted. They tapped on the glass and were surprised when an old woman with skin like the bark of a tree opened the door a crack. When she saw who it was, she let them come in and locked the door behind them.

Again she could hear the whine of a generator somewhere deep underground. It never stopped. It was deep under the cinema. It's probably just because my head aches and my ears are ringing, darling, she thought.

She felt as though she were carrying the whole huge building, as big as a palace, on her shoulders. She'd lost her sense of time and her thoughts had become confused. The things that must have gone on here, she thought. Only I know everything that happened here that night, she thought. But what happened last night? And who knows what will happen during the day? She looked at both unshaven men in their vests of unmatched and hastily sewn together rabbitskins. They'll probably fall apart on their backs, she said to herself.

What is it that tells a person something terrible is about to happen? the old lady asked herself. What is it? Why are we spared nothing? What accumulates all that corrosiveness that eats away at you, telling you something awful is going to happen but you don't know what and wouldn't know, not even if you were to tear yourself apart? Just as she'd felt the weight of the building, with its floors, corridors and staircases, with the cinema and what she'd seen in it, so she felt the weight of the light, the weight of the day, the shadow or echo of what she'd experienced that night. That night? Which night? And her daughter gone without even leaving a message. Where have you gone, my sweet precious one? What pulled you away, my dearest child? She felt as if everything that made people beasts of prey were clinging to her. It was their invention, the Nazi Germans, the word *Menschentiere* or *Tiermenschen*. But it's so close you can reach out and touch it. You don't even have to be a German. They only came close to the ideal, the way they tried to make Saturdays and Sundays into ordinary weekdays. In her mind she saw the employees, the judge, the deserters, the doctor, the general and the colonel, and the people from the NSDAP in the cinema.

She asked the tall fellow and his brother to go out and look for her little girl, her sweet child, her darling, the only thing she had in the world.

"Go, for the love of God," she said, "and find her before something happens to her."

And she thought, oh, my child, I knew you from head to toe, and I'd even find you a cripple for a husband, if only he'd say, "I love you, I'll do everything for you that one person can do for another." She knew that despite her good looks and beautiful hair, her daughter would be capable of finding a legless or armless cripple on a little cart, if only he'd love her and respect her and never desire anyone but her, and she could know he'd never defile her the way the Nazis had defiled the grave of the Unknown Soldier. Where do you get it from, honey? the old woman asked herself.

Aloud she said, "I've never liked this cinema."

"It's a palace," the lanky fellow said.

"I wouldn't live here for all the tea in China," said the cashier's mother.

She looked at the tall fellow and thought: What kind of person are you, living from hand to mouth, forever relying on someone else's favors? Existing without regard for human dignity, without respect for justice, behaving like children who'd renounce their freedom for a glass of lemonade? You'll forget everything, and you'll forgive everything, you pigs.

"You could live in this place for ten years and never set foot outside, that's how big it is," added the lanky fellow's brother. They all knew he meant the owner, who'd bought enough supplies for two weeks and locked himself in his elegant flat, where he'd remain until it was all over.

Both brothers looked at the mother; they appeared to be worried about her. Where should they look for the girl? Do they know something already? the old woman asked herself. Are they trying to keep something from me or do they genuinely not know? And will they really go and look for her?

"There's been shooting again this morning in Parizska Street," said the lanky fellow. "A German armored car was destroyed there, but they say two women were shot."

The lanky fellow's brother looked at the demolished sweetshop across the street. Someone had pulled the metal shutter down over the store front.

"One of their soldiers, a fellow with a raw neck that looks as though they'd tried to hang him, locked an old man up in the projection booth downstairs. The old man's a judge. He sentenced twelve German deserters to death," said the mother.

145

"Downstairs in the cinema?" asked the lanky fellow, surprised.

"But the main one isn't here," said the brother.

"I heard he was shot in front of the Kolovratsky Palace," said the lanky fellow. "I also heard they sent away the soldiers serving under that phony Russian general. Apparently they were wearing half-German uniforms. I couldn't figure for the life of me how they managed that. But if they'd stayed, it might have ended sooner."

"A lot of people kill these days for revenge and even more for money," said the old woman. "There are some days I don't like. Saturday, Monday, and sometimes Tuesday and Wednesday, although Wednesday is usually all right."

"It was a beautiful Saturday, and Sunday and Monday were even better," said the lanky fellow's brother.

The cashier's mother looked sharply at the lanky fellow's brother and thought: They think we're all fallen maidservants that the masters can play with whenever they're in the mood, while the ladies mercifully close their eyes to it all because there are some things that every woman, secretly, is fed up with. Up to her neck. Makes her stomach turn. Many people enter by the side door and go straight to the kitchen. They don't always come through the salon into the dining room. Up the back stairs, so as not to cause a scandal. God, where can you make up for it? Where could I possibly begin to make up for it?

The tall fellow looked at the sausage stand, now closed and covered with a sheet of canvas, and thought of the man who owned it: For the whole war you tasted good, hot meat, not like my brother here, who sold newspapers and was worn away by tuberculosis.

A fire will come and destroy all of it, thought the lanky fellow's brother. It will sweep away what used to be to make room for what is yet to come. Sonitschka Vagnerova. She should have lived to see it, she should at least have lived to see it. But perhaps she could imagine it for a brief moment before she began to suffocate and tear at herself with her fingernails. At first it may have seemed that she had a chance, but as it turned out, those who had less chance than you, Sonitschka Vagnerova, survived. They say that some Jewish survivors have already reached Prague. They hustled them into some hospitals or hotels. They must have been running like that famous guy at Marathon. Only no one was starving him along the way, or gassing him or hanging him, or taking shots at him at every step. And for them it was a hundred times farther. Nor did these people carry any victorious message.

"What's going on out there?" asked the old woman.

"Their general asked for air support," replied the lanky fellow. "Near the radio building, one of their women with only a brassiere on was firing a machine gun all night from a balcony on the top floor. They made a nest there. When they picked her off with a grenade from the roof, her son came out of the flat and took over, but he got it, too. He was scarcely thirteen. At the general hospital kids like that were shooting at pedestrians from the emergency room."

"Only birds have nests," said the mother. "I was always afraid of that. But I believed we'd live to see the unknown day together. And what comes afterwards, too."

"You should go and lie down, lady. You can hardly keep your eyes open," said the lanky fellow.

Human eyes are too weak for all that evil, thought his brother. He looked at his stolen boots from the Afrika Korps, and when he saw the old lady looking at them, too, he explained: "They belonged to a rat we stripped everything off of. It sounds like there's a river roaring through the basement here, lady."

"The underground newspapers wrote that Reinhard Eugen Tristan Heydrich was a passionate airman before they blew him up with a grenade. He wouldn't let a Czech doctor treat him, and by the time they found a German doctor, it was too late. Hitler got angry because the two of them were hand in glove and he eventually wanted Heydrich to take his place if anything happened to him. But he was lucky," added the lanky fellow. "Nothing much ever happened to him, except that he couldn't write without his right hand shaking and trembling. They say Benito Mussolini was a passionate airman, too. And the members of his family were passionate airmen; his daughter Edita, wife of the Count Cian, and his sons, Captain Vittorio and Bruno, who were combat pilots in the Ethiopian campaign and the Spanish war, which is where they won their wings and their ranks. Maybe what we're hearing right now are passionate airmen at work. The last of their passionate airmen."

He thought: It has given strength to many who were weak. It has given back a bit of good conscience to those who were tarnished. But people like the owner of the cinema and the sausage seller will try to go

147

on living like parasites in the future. Many of them will slip through. But we'll know who they are, he thought.

"Leave me a box of matches," said the mother suddenly to the lanky fellow.

"Sure," said the tall fellow, handing them to her. "But you'll have to get your own candles."

"What else have you seen?" asked the old woman. It still seemed to her that generators were whining somewhere underground. But it must be in my head, too, she concluded.

"I only saw the evacuation. On the left bank of the Vltava the Revolutionary Guard gave them passes. The condition was that they had to surrender their heavy arms at the Prague city limits. They are allowed to take small arms with them on their way to give themselves up to the Americans. They believe the Americans will forgive them, that everything will quickly be forgotten, just like after the First World War. For those who went, they opened the barricades a single tank width. But they had to leave their tanks behind, empty. Yesterday, they tied our people to the gun barrels of those tanks and said they'd blast them to bits if we didn't stop pouring gasoline on them. But the line was so long I was amazed we were able to hold out against them at all. They have reserves in the barracks and they're covering their retreat. They have armored cars, cannons and tanks, trucks full of machine gun brigades, hundreds of trucks and cars. And civilians are bringing up the rear on foot, as if they were following the Pied Piper. There isn't enough room for them all in the trucks. They were running alongside, tying baby carriages to the trucks and then they ran behind to keep up, all covered with sweat like in those underground mines in Venezuela, my brother says. I'm almost beginning to believe it. They're terrified, shrunken, sick with fear, dragging their personal junk behind them. And there are sick people and children among them. Women with bundles on their backs. They don't want to lose sight of the one column of soldiers they have, otherwise there would be no one to protect them. It looks like the last armed units they have, lady."

"What day is it, anyway?" asked the cashier's mother.

"This is the fifth day you've been here, mother," said the lanky fellow. "Tuesday."

"The fifth day, Tuesday, and my little girl still isn't with me," said the mother. "If only I could turn it around."

"Love has no frontiers," said the lanky fellow's brother.

148

"Love?" asked the old woman spitefully. "Only the instinct to survive has no frontiers."

She was looking at both brothers and thought: How many times have you helped an old woman board a tram, my dear brothers? As far as I remember, you haven't helped me even once. How many times have you walked unconcerned past cripples, beggars, deserted mothers with babies? Isn't it like this with you always? Won't the one who won't burn his fingers have a greater chance to survive than the one who sticks his nose into other people's business?

"People watched like in a theater," added the lanky fellow. "Crowds of people. Like when there's an accident or a fire. They poured out into the streets from nowhere, God knows where. Since Saturday the streets were empty, and suddenly—it was an amazing show. And it's not over yet."

"I remember people staring out the windows across from the Holesovice-Bubny train station at the Jewish transports when they were collecting for departure," he went on. "Like a show in a theater. And now they're watching the Germans. As long as they have something to watch. You're telling me this is all a theater for people? Folks were staring at Jewish families while they still were allowed to ride the back platform on the streetcars. And when they crowded together at the Radio Market Hall of the Grand Fair Palace. It was a wonder people didn't applaud like in the theater. They were saying to themselves: It serves them right. To see those fat cats carrying sacks, dragging along two-wheel carts. A circus. They'd been living too good for too long. They envied them even the noses between their eyes; otherwise the Germans couldn't have gotten away with it that easily, after all. Before the Gestapo sealed their apartments, the servants would stretch their arms out and run their feet off, carrying away as much Jewish property as possible."

"People always like to watch when it's turning around," said the lanky fellow. And he thought: Perhaps you were watching, too, old woman. "Tomorrow is also a day, lady. You know what that priest used to say: 'God will take care of the impossible things. We'll take care of the possible things ourselves.' "

"I hope so."

"Don't panic, lady. Don't give in to it. It's better to feel sorry for all the other people than for yourself. The wild dog has to be kept on a short leash. Sometimes more happens in a day than in a year. My grandpa used to say that if you can last till you're nineteen and don't drown till you're twenty, you won't get lost anymore.''

The old woman looked out of bloodshot eyes full of the sleep she had denied herself for so many days. Maybe it was five days already, she thought, five days, my dearest sweetheart. Well, we weren't alive yet, my darling. Only now will we start living. It's all still waiting for you. Your life is ahead of you. I'm on my last legs. I love you, little girl, even though you're rebellious. I was at your age. I don't want you to be gentle like a lamb. You can believe me. I accept you as you are. It has begun for you, and these are not good times.

''I could tell guilt from innocence Saturday, Sunday, or any day of the week,'' said the tall fellow's brother. ''When the final reckoning comes, I won't let anyone leave out Sonitschka Vagnerova, no matter what day it is. That's if anyone were to ask me how the whole world could stay sitting at the table and have Sunday dinner and Sunday supper and allow what we allowed to happen.''

''She never let me wait for her this long, like a blind woman,'' said the mother. ''So this is the wonderful day.''

''Only those who actually did something wrong are evil,'' said the lanky fellow's brother. And he was thinking that before they asphyxiated Sonitschka Vagnerova with Zyklon-B, they suffocated her with silence. They wanted their *Lebensraum,* and they suffocated her to make more room. They used words like *Ausrotten, Vernichtung durch Arbeit.*

''You should take a rest,'' said the lanky fellow to the mother.

''We're all prematurely worn out,'' said his brother. He looked at the posters with the stars of pre-war films.

''You said there was shooting in Parizska Street. What happened there? Did they kill anyone?''

''Yes, two women. But that doesn't mean anything,'' added the lanky fellow quickly. ''It's just a rumor. We didn't actually see it happen.''

''What would I do if they killed her? Where are you, my sweet little girl?'' asked the old woman. The thought startled her. I mustn't bring down bad luck, my darling, she thought.

She wished her daughter would come to her, and she had other thoughts as well.

''The sausage man closed up shop,'' said the tall fellow. ''All he said was that on Friday they bought his sausages and Saturday morning they got a shot of phenol in the heart. On Sunday they don't bury the dead.

The newspapers said the stags have already shed their antlers. What were they trying to say?"

"The same as what Sonitschka Vagnerova was trying to say, that's all," said the brother.

"They're probably cut off from the world, in their own little nests," said the lanky fellow.

"What nests do you mean? Those aren't nests," the mother corrected him. "They don't even live like animals. They don't understand anything. They're worse than a storm. They've gone wild. I was always afraid of what would happen when that day arrived. We always did everything together. Why did she leave by herself?"

"Don't worry about it," said the lanky fellow

"What would Sonitschka Vagnerova have said?" asked his brother.

The mother's look could have penetrated a stone. A bitter dampness filled her eyes. "She always clung so close to me," she said again.

"It'll all turn out for the best," said the lanky fellow.

"I'm afraid," repeated the mother. "I'm afraid of everything now, even my own shadow. Of sickness, of being alone. That I won't last. Oh, my God, what would I do alone?"

"You see, when they were wiping out people like Sonitschka Vagnerova, they weren't able to wipe out their names," said the brother. "When I had that fever on Thursday and God appeared to me, I realized why only this will give people back their tarnished honor and allow the humiliated to walk straight again. But only those who sacrifice themselves and don't try to drive out evil with evil, hatred with hatred, will be spared, or will spare others. And we won't let it get out of hand. Every one of them who murdered will work in the deepest mine shafts of Venezuela, with no respite. And those who were murdered will live on and their names will be with us."

The mother absentmindedly rearranged her dress, covering her ankles with the edge of her skirt. It's easy for you to talk, she thought. You have teeth that could tear a rabbit to pieces. And eyes that see only what they want to see.

It's 9:30, she thought, and it's still cool, even though it's May and the elders are blooming and the lilacs are fragrant. There's a dampness coming off the river. I can feel it when the wind blows through the passageway.

The old woman had hard eyes like the lanky fellow's brother's dog in winter. They were indifferent and cold. They had shadows, reading as deep as a dark well and yet as shallow as a dry field.

"It's cold. The furnaces aren't working," said the lanky fellow.

"We have to go," said the brother. "A few people have to sacrifice themselves and get dirt on their hands so the others won't have to corrupt themselves with all that evil."

"Your eyes are red; you should rest," said the tall fellow.

10

The cashier's mother waited until evening. Then it was eleven o'clock and her daughter hadn't reappeared all that time she was dressed like a widow, wearing black from boots to collar. She stopped the ceaseless inner conversations in which she tried to persuade her daughter not to get mixed up in any mob activity. They've killed her, she repeated. Wolves are always just wolves. Wolves will never change. Why didn't you listen to me, my angel, little girl, when I told you about the shadows that follow you everywhere? My sweet rain-frog, my precious jewel.

She talked to no one, looked at no one. She tried to walk erect and resolute, the way she had when she was young, coming home through the streets in the early morning as it was getting light and when, despite everything, she felt young and healthy. Young and healthy, my girl, she repeated.

The soldier with the raw neck that suggested a last-minute reprieve from the gallows was holding onto the cord of the dark blue velvet curtain and looking through the little window into the projection booth where he'd locked up the old Nazi judge like a rat. He didn't know what to do next.

She walked by him without a word. Maybe she saw him as he crouched there in the light of a single candle. For the past few days the judge had eaten only bread crusts and dry cookies the soldier with the raw neck had tossed to him.

She looked through the window beside the circular opening through which the lens of the huge projector stared like the eye of a dead fish. The bodies of some of the murdered soldiers were lying on the floor.

The old man had hairy arms and the skin on the back of his hands was covered with dark blotches. His shirt sleeves, visible under his hunting jacket, were no longer clean. His jaw was sunken and his eyes were streaming with tears. He must have been thirsty because his mouth was partially open and he occasionally thrust his tongue between his lips. A set of dentures had fallen out of his mouth and lay on the floor. His teeth and gums had turned yellow. Around the fly of his trousers there were yellow stains. He was terrified of what the deserter with the raw neck might do, but he hadn't been beaten.

"You rat," said the mother. "You plague." So this is my unknown day—the day of the animal, not the day of victory. What can I do to make up for it, since you didn't come back to me? Nothing, nothing, or little, if I can find the strength, and I'll do the only thing I can, something I should have done long ago, when you were still with me.

She was talking to herself while she took the lid off the cannister of gasoline. She poured the gasoline through the small window onto the old man. He was terrified and retreated into a corner, stepping on his false teeth and crushing them. Then she poured the rest through the window and watched it spread across the floor. Even in the gloom the gasoline made small rainbow eyes. It ran into a large pool on the floor and it smelled very strong. She took a match, struck it and tossed it through the window. Something was telling the old woman not to do it. But it was only a vibration, a heartbeat, the wink of a swollen eyelid, the look of fatigued eyes. It became an echo before an idea—a breath, a word which would reverse what she was committing, many yeses and only one no which she didn't hear anymore. She was looking at the old man's face and, in it, suddenly discovered the reason she didn't like herself anymore.

Saliva was running down from the corners of her mouth. Am I punishing myself for what doesn't cleanse one, doesn't redeem one, doesn't help anyone? The good ones will die, the bad ones remain, she was repeating to herself. How can I live? How will I live? She sensed a dark connection between her memory and that which carried her name, her countenance, looked through her eyes, spoke her language. I have lived long. Why?

She was pale, with deep circles under her eyes, like people whose hearts are sick and who have lost respect for the world and for themselves; who have lost the awareness of their own worth. With an absent expression and her mouth slightly ajar, the old woman closed her eyes. Right without God, she was whispering. Justice without God. Or is it the other way around, God without Justice? You will tell, my little one. You'll see.

Her whispers were unintelligible. First the pool of gasoline caught fire and was covered by a blue flame that was reddish in the middle. Then the flames spread. The old man in the hunter's jacket and plus fours began to shriek. He sounded like a child crying.

The mother sank to her knees so she couldn't see what was going on in the projection booth. The fire cast rays of light on her only when the flames were high enough, ruddy reflections that became brighter as the darkness in the empty cinema deepened. She knelt as though she were praying, but she wasn't praying. The old man in the booth cried out hoarsely. She had colored reflections in her eyes, red explosions that shot outwards. Suddenly they became yellow and finally black, like the smoke that now enveloped her.

In her mind the old lady spoke to herself, but at the same time, she addressed her lost daughter: It had to come, to him, to all of them. Her mouth stiffened. She could no longer speak, not even to herself. Her lips became encrusted, as though the fire had already scorched them. Then she began to cough and choke and she closed her eyes, which were streaming with tears.

She felt nothing when the soldier with the raw neck dragged her away and she heard familiar voices, because the fire from the burning door had already reached her.

Afterword by
Josef Škvorecký

A RNOŠT Lustig is certainly one of the most remarkable writers whose imagination has been shaped by the experience of the Holocaust. If he is less known internationally than others, it is because he writes in that minor Slavic language called Czech which, in the awareness of many people in the West, has only recently been connected with works of high literary art. But he is not a remarkable writer only because he depicts the Jewish tragedy better than most; he is remarkable because the tragedy of a specific people becomes, in his fiction, the tragedy of man. And that, to my mind, is the sign of great literature.

Lustig burst on the Czech literary scene at the end of the fifties, during the last days of the reign of Stalin's ill-conceived child called socialist realism. The stories of *Night and Hope (Noc a naděje*, 1958) came as a literary revelation for they bore no traces of that mandatory formula. Although mostly about death and dying, these stories were filled with an intense feeling of life, fleeting, tragic, maddeningly brief—in short, human. They—and other stories and short novels that followed—became one of the landmarks of contemporary Czech fiction bearing witness to the *situation humaine,* and refused to be subservient to the official political and aesthetic powers. Lustig's name, in the minds of his many Czech readers (by no means all Jews, of which, after all, only a handful were left in Czechoslovakia after the era of the gas chambers) is linked with the names of other shapers of true modern fiction such as Milan Kundera, Ota Pavel, Ludvík Vaculík, Jiří Gruša, Ivan Klíma, etc. They all were a group of friends who together inaugurated the age of promise, cut short by another Holocaust, this time mostly spiritual, that overcame Lustig's native land after the Soviet invasion of 1968. As many others—Jews and non-Jews—he had to leave the beloved country for the land that, no matter how confusingly complex and often mistaken, is still humanity's land of promise—the United States of America.

Like other creative men and women of his generation, Lustig had been deprived of formal education by the Nazi disaster. But he studied with passion the great literary masters of Czech literature and of Jewish literature written in Bohemia, both in Czech (Karel Poláček) and in German (Franz Kafka); he was also fascinated by the magical techniques of William Faulkner, whose works appeared in Czech translation during Lustig's formative period in the mid-fifties. He applied the lessons learned from these diverse artists to his own unique tragic experience. His were the first stories about Hell in Czech literature written with literary mastership. They were followed by other works, some written on non-Jewish themes and daringly critical of the political practices of the Czech government, such as *White Birch Trees in Autumn (Bílé břízy na podzim,* 1966), some based on the Jewish experience, such as *A Prayer for Katerina Horovitzhova (Modlitba pro Kateřinu Horovitzovou,* 1964), perhaps the finest short novel to have come out of Bohemia about the suffering of the innocent. His stories became the material for such outstanding Czech films of the New Wave (and Lustig was one of the most important screenwriters of that celebrated movement) as Jan Němec's *Diamonds of the Night (Démanty noci,* 1964) or Zbyněk Brynych's *Transport from Paradise (Transport z ráje,* 1962).

Indecent Dreams is a step forward in Lustig's literary development. The heroines of the three novellas are not Jews—although the Jewish tragedy is always present in the background and seeps through to the surface in memories of Jewish friends or lovers that haunt the minds of the Czech and German protagonists. These stories are studies of the *Götterdämmerung;* of the last days of the war, psychological probings into the souls of the hardened Nazis now at the end of their tether; of simple-minded Germans who, without thinking, made hay of the opportunities that the liquidation of the Jews brought them; and of Czechs who lived through the dusk of the war with a mixture of hope, yearning for revenge, and revulsion at the butchery that marked those last days of the man-made inferno. The author, with great effect and a deep understanding for the real workings of the human soul, merges the outside and the inside of the human being, employing a technique that is basically filmic but, in contrast to film, makes use of the specific possibilities of fiction: instrospection, the landscape of the mind. The stories marvelously succeed in creating a canvas of hysteria in which the bloody events blend with very private thoughts and dreams that seemingly have nothing in common with events in the objective world. Very few stories in world literature express so vividly the madness in the minds of people living on the brink of death so close to peace and life. Scene after scene evokes the images of life far removed from what human life should be: the execution by injection of the German deserters on the eve of peace; the claustrophobic atmosphere of the apartment where a German woman is hiding a Nazi judge; the senseless death of a Czech girl who witnesses the destruction of a German tank on Prague's Old Town Square. These scenes are truly unforgettable, unlike anything in the vast bulk of war literature. They unveil a little-known aspect of the great killing, rendered humanely and with supreme artistry.